# Kiss My Grits, Sugar

## Southern Humor
## with a Side of Tasty Fixin's

## Gloria Hander Lyons

**Blue Sage Press**

# Kiss My Grits, Sugar
Southern Humor
with a Side of Tasty Fixin's

Inquires should be addressed to:
Blue Sage Press
48 Borondo Pines
La Marque, TX 77568
www.BlueSagePress.com

ISBN: 978-0-9842438-3-9

Library of Congress Control Number: 2010907908

First Edition: June 2010

Printed in the United States of America

*This book is dedicated to my mama,
Iva Nell Owens, and her mama,
Anna Bell O'Daniel, for making me
the Mama I am today.*

\* \* \* \* \* \*

*Many thanks to my neighbor,
Kathy Goodwin, for providing
the inspiration for this book.*

*Here's a heads-up for those of you who know me and my kin. Don't go gettin' your feathers all ruffled over these stories 'cause they're pure dee fiction—for the most part.*

# Table of Contents

# Kiss My Grits, Sugar

## Introduction

Being a food lover all my life, I've been collecting and testing recipes ever since I was knee-high to a grasshopper. My fondness for cooking (and eating) eventually teamed up with my desire to share my recipes, so I began writing cookbooks.

So far I've penned twelve tomes on various cooking topics, but not a single one on Southern cuisine. I do declare! As my mama asked me many times, "Gloria Jean, don't you have a lick of sense?"

Since I'm a Southern girl through and through—born in Louisiana and raised in Texas, I reckon it's high time I got around to writing a book filled with good old Southern recipes. My mouth is watering just thinking about fried chicken, potato salad, banana pudding and pecan pie. This book is chock full of my family's favorites.

And because I'm not the serious type, I like my food served up with some humor on the side. So I tucked in a few tall tales from my childhood about me and my kin that I hope will tickle your funny bone.

Most books by Southern women, about Southern women, carry on and on about the endless rules imposed on those pathetic creatures—never wear white shoes after Labor Day, never use dark meat in your chicken salad, and never, ever forget to send thank you notes.

My poor mama, bless her heart, she tried, but I never took kindly to following a bunch of senseless rules. For small-town Southern Baptist girls, my two sisters and I were a pretty feisty lot—traditional belles we were not.

Now, don't get me wrong. My Southern roots are deep and Southern cooking is about as good as it gets, but when I was told to mind my manners or else, my response was, "Kiss my grits!"

# Learning the Hard Way

From an early age, Southern girls are taught never to swear. But everyone knows swearing is just a way of letting off steam when you get your feathers ruffled. Out of necessity, we've invented a few colorful expletives over time to help vent our anger without offending those in polite society.

One morning when I was eight, and my two sisters were six and ten, we gathered around the kitchen table to eat our usual hearty breakfast of eggs, biscuits, jam, bacon and grits. Since I enjoyed experimenting with my food, I stirred a bit of sugar into my grits.

My older sister, Anna, was horrified. "Gloria Jean, don't you have a grain of sense? You're not supposed to put sugar in grits!"

"I'll eat my grits any way I want and if you don't like it you can kiss my...!"

Both my sisters sucked in air. "Don't you dare say a cuss word!" Anna said.

I scooped up a big spoonful of grits and flicked it in her direction. "Kiss my grits!" I yelled.

The white mush landed with a splat just above her left eye. She growled and returned fire with a forkful of eggs-over-easy.

"Quit it!" snapped my younger sister, Charlotte. "Mama's gonna have a hissy fit when she sees this mess!"

Two biscuits bounced off the top of her head. "Mama!" she wailed.

By the time our mama showed up, Anna and I were locked in a death grip, rolling around on the floor, and covered head to toe in food.

Needless to say, the two of us spent the rest of the morning sweeping and mopping the floor, scrubbing the table and washing the dishes while Charlotte played in the backyard.

"I hope you've learned your lesson," said Mama after we'd put away the last of the clean dishes.

"Yes, Ma'am," we said in unison.

We learned our lesson all right. Next time we'd settle our differences outside.

# Old-Fashioned Southern Grits

Grits are coarsely ground dried corn, and are simple to make, but if you're in a hurry, you can use instant or "quick cooking" grits. Grits are a traditional Southern dish, usually served with breakfast.

4 cups water
1 teaspoon salt
1 cup grits
1/4 cup butter or margarine

In a large saucepan, bring the water to a boil. Add salt. Stir in grits. Cover and cook on low 20-25 minutes, stirring frequently. (Don't let them burn!). Remove from heat and stir in butter.

# Cheesy Grits

2 cups milk
2 cups water
1 teaspoon salt
1 cup regular grits
1/4 teaspoon ground black pepper
1/4 cup butter
1 cup (4 ozs.) shredded Cheddar cheese

Place the milk, water, and salt into a large saucepan. Cook over medium-high heat until boiling. Gradually add grits, stirring constantly. Decrease the heat to low and cover. Stir frequently, every 3 to 4 minutes, to prevent grits from sticking or forming lumps. Cook 20 to 25 minutes or until mixture is creamy. Remove from the heat. Stir in pepper and butter. Gradually stir in the cheese a little at a time, until melted.

# Shrimp and Grits

4 cups water
1 teaspoon salt
1 cup regular grits
3 tablespoons butter
2 cups shredded sharp cheddar cheese
1 pound shrimp, peeled and deveined
6 slices bacon
1 tablespoon lemon juice
2 tablespoons chopped parsley
1/2 cup thinly sliced green onions
1 clove garlic, finely minced

Bring water to a boil. Stir in salt and grits. Reduce heat to low, cover and cook, stirring frequently, for about 20 to 25 minutes. Remove from heat and stir in butter and cheese.

Rinse shrimp and pat dry. Fry bacon in a large skillet until browned; remove, drain and crumble. Add shrimp to hot grease; cook just until shrimp turn pink. Add lemon juice, parsley, onion and garlic. Sauté for about 3 minutes. Stir in crumbled bacon.

Serve cooked shrimp over grits.

# Mama's Homemade Biscuits

2 cups all purpose flour
2 teaspoons baking powder
1/4 teaspoon baking soda
2 teaspoons salt
1/2 cup vegetable shortening
1 cup buttermilk*

Preheat oven to 450°.

In a large bowl, combine flour, baking powder, baking soda and salt.

Cut in shortening using two knives or a pastry blender until the mixture is crumbly.

Add buttermilk, stirring until you have a sticky dough. Turn out onto a lightly floured surface. Gently flatten to a thickness of about 3/4 of an inch. Cut out using a biscuit cutter. Place biscuits on a lightly greased cookie sheet and bake until tops are a golden brown (about 10-12 minutes).

Makes about 8-10 biscuits, depending on the size of your biscuit cutter.

**Note:** Mama used to melt 2-3 tablespoons of bacon drippings in a baking pan in the oven. She placed each biscuit in the pan, then turned it over, coating the biscuits on both sides before baking them.

*If you don't have buttermilk, stir 1 tablespoon lemon juice or white vinegar into enough milk to equal 1 cup. Let stand for at least 5 minutes.

# Sausage Gravy

1/2 pound bulk pork sausage
1/4 cup chopped onion
1/4 cup bacon grease
2-4 tablespoons all purpose flour
Milk
Salt and pepper to taste

In a small skillet, cook the sausage and onion over medium-high heat until sausage is done; drain fat.

In a large skillet, heat the bacon grease over medium heat. Stir in flour, one tablespoon at a time to make roux, until you have the consistency of a runny paste. Cook, stirring constantly until the roux is lightly browned.

Stir in about 1/2 cup of milk and cook, stirring constantly until gravy begins to thicken. Continue to add milk a little at a time, cooking until it thickens and you have the gravy at the consistency you like.

Add the cooked sausage and onion mixture and salt and pepper to taste. Cook until heated through.

Serve over split, hot biscuits.

# Electrified

As a child, I was a never-ending source of grief for my mama. Not only was I a tomboy, but my curiosity more often than not landed me in a whole heap of trouble.

One afternoon, when I was four, Mama invited our neighbor over for a visit. They sat in two comfy chairs in the living room, drinking coffee and eating one of Mama's favorite company desserts while they chatted.

For no particular reason, I got a notion to climb up on the floor lamp that stood between their two chairs. It had a sturdy wooden pole with three lights under a barrel shade at the top.

I shimmied up the pole and discovered the hard way that one of the light sockets was missing a bulb.

Every light in the house flickered while the electric current took a detour through me. My muscles contracted so tight I thought my bones would break. But, no matter how hard I tried, I couldn't let go of that pole.

Mama danced around, screaming like a banshee. Thank God the neighbor had the good sense to unplug the lamp cord before I turned to toast.

My body dropped to the floor, limp as a dishrag. I felt like one of Mama's fried pies. I swear my hair smelled like it was singed all the way to the roots.

After checking to see that I was still breathing, Mama was beside herself. She couldn't decide whether to give me a whippin' for scaring the bejeezus out of her or console me with a pile of my favorite cookies.

The cookies finally won out—I reckon she knew there'd be plenty more opportunities in my future for whippin's.

Overall, I wasn't too worse for the wear—my brain didn't seem to be any more scrambled than usual. But we had the dickens of a time trying to get my hair to stay down. Mama finally tied a scarf around my head so I wouldn't keep scaring the dog.

I steered clear of electrical appliances for a long spell after that electrifying experience. And to this very day, I'm fanatical about keeping all the light sockets filled with bulbs—whether they work or not.

# Fried Fruit Pies

1 (21-oz.) can fruit pie filling of your choice
Vegetable oil for frying

Pastry recipe (makes twelve 5- to 6-inch pies):
3 cups all-purpose flour
1 teaspoon salt
3/4 cup vegetable shortening
1 egg, lightly beaten
1/4 cup cold water
1 teaspoon white vinegar

In a large bowl, blend flour and salt. Cut in shortening with a pastry blender or two knives, until mixture resembles coarse crumbs. In a separate bowl, stir together egg, water and vinegar. Add to flour mixture, mixing lightly, until ingredients are well combined. Form dough into a ball and wrap in plastic wrap. Refrigerate for at least one hour.

Divide pastry dough into 12 golf-size balls. Roll out each one on a lightly floured surface into a 5" or 6" circle. Place 2 rounded tablespoons of fruit pie filling on one side of the circle. Wet the edges of the pastry circle with your finger dipped in water, fold circle in half, enclosing the pie filling and press edges to seal. Use a fork to crimp the edges, if desired.

In a large frying pan, heat about 1/2" of vegetable oil until hot (about 375º). Cook pies until golden brown on each side. Remove from pan and drain on paper towels.

Optional: Dust pies with powdered sugar or drizzle with glaze made by blending 1 cup powdered sugar with just enough milk or water to make drizzling consistency. Serve pies warm.

# Fresh Apple Cake

2 cups granulated sugar
1 cup vegetable oil
3 large eggs
2 teaspoons vanilla extract
3 cups all-purpose flour
1/4 teaspoon salt
1 teaspoon baking soda
2 teaspoons ground cinnamon
3 cups peeled and diced apples
1 cup chopped pecans

Preheat oven to 325°. Grease and flour a 12-cup tube pan or Bundt pan.

In a large bowl, beat together sugar, oil, eggs and vanilla. In a separate bowl, mix flour, salt, baking soda and cinnamon.

Stir flour mixture into egg mixture. Add apples and pecans; stir until well blended. Pour batter into prepared pan.

Bake about 1 hour and 15 minutes or until done. Cool in pan on wire rack for 15 minutes before removing. Invert cake onto wire rack to cool completely.

# Zucchini Bread

1 cup grated zucchini (about 1 large)
1 cup granulated sugar
1/2 cup vegetable oil
1 teaspoon vanilla extract
2 eggs
1-1/2 cups all-purpose flour
1 teaspoon ground cinnamon
1/2 teaspoon salt
1/2 teaspoon baking powder
1/2 teaspoon baking soda
1/2 cup chopped pecans

Preheat oven to 350°.

In a large mixing bowl, combine zucchini, sugar, oil, vanilla extract and eggs. Beat until well blended.

In a separate bowl, mix flour, cinnamon, salt, baking powder and baking soda.

Stir into the zucchini mixture. Fold in pecans.

Pour into a 9" x 5" x 3" greased and floured loaf pan. Bake 55-60 minutes or until done. Remove from pan and cool on wire rack.

# Cowboy Cookies

2 cups all-purpose flour
1 teaspoon ground cinnamon
1 teaspoon baking soda
1/2 teaspoon salt
1/2 teaspoon baking powder
1 cup butter, softened
1 cup granulated sugar
1 cup brown sugar, packed
2 large eggs
1 teaspoon vanilla extract
2 cups old-fashioned rolled oats
1/2 cup chopped pecans
1 (6-oz.) package chocolate chips
1/2 cup shredded coconut, packed

Preheat oven to 350°.

In a large bowl, mix together flour, cinnamon, baking soda, salt, and baking powder.

In a separate bowl, cream butter, granulated sugar and brown sugar. Add eggs and vanilla and beat until well blended. On low speed, beat in flour mixture. Add oats, nuts, chocolate chips and coconut. Mix well.

Drop by rounded tablespoonfuls onto greased cookie sheet about 3" apart. Bake for 15-18 minutes, or until edges begin to brown. Do not over bake.

Transfer cookies to a wire rack to cool.

# Something to Crow About

One Easter, when my sisters and I were ages four, six and eight, our Granny O'Daniel surprised us with a live baby chick. We named her Jenny. That poor critter actually managed to survive our affectionate squeezes and constant petting.

Before too long, our cute little pink chick grew into a big, white rooster. We changed his name to Jake. He was ruler of the roost, and mean as the dickens. Jake laid claim to the back yard and viciously attacked anyone who dared enter his domain.

When Mama carted the laundry out to the wash house or tried to hang clothes on the clothes line to dry, that rooster chased after her—pecking at her heels. Mama kicked and cussed at that bird the whole way.

My sisters and I stayed clear of the back yard. We played out front on our swing set. One day, my younger sister, Charlotte, jumped off the swing and let out a blood-curdling scream. "It's Jake!" she yelled. "He got out of the fence."

"Run!" said my older sister, Anna. "Get to the house!"

We sprinted towards the house with Jake angrily flapping his wings and snapping at our bare legs. I tripped and fell face down in the grass. He jumped on my head, pulling at my hair with his stubby beak.

"Get up!" yelled Anna.

"I can't," I screeched. "He won't get off!"

Mama barreled out of the house wielding a long-handled broom. She batted that monster off my head and yanked me to my feet. "Run!" she yelled. "Get in the house!"

We all tumbled through the door and slammed it behind us. Mamma grabbed the phone and called her daddy, "Come get this crazy rooster!" she said.

"You're scared that that little critter?" he scoffed.

Mama just smiled and raised a knowing eyebrow.

When Grandpa O'Daniel drove up in his truck, we glued ourselves to the front window. He sauntered over to the truck bed, gave us a wink and a friendly wave and pulled out a small wire cage.

Out of nowhere, Jake pounced on his arm and began pecking Grandpa's hand. He dropped the cage and shook the bird off. Jake jumped up again and dug his claws into Grandpa's knee.

Grandpa fought to pull Jake off, but he stumbled backwards and tripped over the cage. Jake had the upper hand now. He fluttered up to Grandpa's chest, furiously attacking his face.

Grandpa looked like a windmill, trying to bat that crazed bird off his chest. He grabbed Jake around the neck, stuffed him into the cage and dropped the cage into the truck bed.

We all breathed a collective sigh of relief. But Grandpa's cocky smile had turned into a scowl. He pulled out his handkerchief and wiped the sweat from his brow. It's a good thing we couldn't hear the language he spewed as he slammed the truck door and backed out of the driveway.

Mama just smiled and gave him a wink and a friendly wave.

# Southern Fried Chicken

1 (3-pound) frying chicken, cut into 8 pieces
2 cups buttermilk
1 large onion, sliced
1 teaspoon dried parsley flakes
1/2 teaspoon paprika
1/4 teaspoon cayenne pepper
2 cups all-purpose flour
1/2 teaspoon garlic powder
1 teaspoon paprika
1/2 teaspoon cayenne pepper (or to taste)
1 teaspoon salt
2 cups shortening or peanut oil

Soak chicken overnight or at least 8 hours in buttermilk with onions, parsley, 1/2 teaspoon paprika and 1/4 teaspoon cayenne pepper. Drain.

In a large paper (or plastic) bag, mix flour with garlic powder, 1 teaspoon paprika, 1/2 teaspoon cayenne and salt.

Heat about 2 cups of oil in a large, heavy-bottomed skillet (cast iron is best) on medium high heat until a pinch of flour starts to sizzle when dropped in the hot oil (about 350°).

Place chicken pieces in bag with flour and shake until thoroughly coated. Add chicken to hot oil and fry on one side for 12-15 minutes, until golden brown. Use tongs to turn pieces over and fry for another 10-12 minutes, or until done. Fry chicken pieces in small batches; overcrowding will drop the temperature of the oil too quickly and the chicken will be soggy.

Use tongs to remove chicken from pan. Place on a rack over a cookie sheet to drain the excess oil.

# Chicken and Dumplings

These are Mama's light and fluffy dumplings that cook on top of the chicken stew.

2 cups, chopped, cooked chicken
3 tablespoons butter or margarine
1/2 cup chopped onion
1/2 cup chopped celery
3 tablespoons all-purpose flour
1 teaspoon salt
1/8 teaspoon ground black pepper
1 cup chicken broth
   (or use 2 teaspoons chicken bouillon granules
    dissolved in 1 cup hot water)
1 cup milk
1 cup frozen peas and carrots
2 cups biscuit baking mix
1 tablespoon dried parsley flakes
1/4 teaspoon poultry seasoning
2/3 cup milk

In a large saucepan, melt butter and sauté onions and celery over medium heat until tender. Blend in flour, salt and pepper. Cook for 1 minute. Stir in chicken broth and 1 cup milk. Bring to a boil, stirring constantly until slightly thickened. Stir in chicken and peas and carrots. Heat to boiling over low heat.

To make dumplings: Stir together 2 cups baking mix, parsley, poultry seasoning and 2/3 cup milk to form a soft dough. Drop by rounded teaspoonfuls onto boiling chicken mixture. Cook uncovered over low heat 10 minutes; cover and cook 10 minutes longer or until dumplings are done. Makes four servings.

# Chicken Salad

2 cups diced cooked chicken
1/3 cup mayonnaise
1/3 cup sour cream
1 cup seedless red grapes, halved
1/2 cup thinly sliced celery
1/2 cup coarsely chopped pecans
2 tablespoons minced green onion, with some
    green tops
Salt and ground black pepper to taste
Salad greens, optional

In a large bowl, combine chicken with mayonnaise, sour cream, grapes, green onions, celery, pecans, salt, and pepper. Cover and chill until ready to serve.

Serve on salad greens, if desired. For sandwiches, line sandwich rolls with lettuce leaves and fill with chicken salad.

# Smothered Chicken

1 whole chicken, cut into 8 pieces
1 cup, plus 1 tablespoon all-purpose flour
Salt and ground black pepper to taste
1/2 cup vegetable oil
1 cup chopped onion
1 cup chopped green bell pepper
1/2 cup chopped celery
1 cup water
1 teaspoon chicken bouillon granules (optional)
Hot cooked rice (optional)

Sprinkle chicken pieces with salt and pepper. Season 1 cup of the flour with salt and pepper. Dredge chicken pieces in flour mixture until coated on all sides. Shake off any excess flour.

Heat the vegetable oil in a large skillet over medium-high heat. Add chicken pieces and brown on all sides. Remove chicken pieces to drain.

Pour off all but 2 tablespoons of drippings from the skillet. Reduce heat to medium. Add the onions, peppers and celery to the skillet and cook, stirring frequently, until tender. Remove vegetables.

Sprinkle 1 tablespoon of flour in skillet. Cook until golden brown, stirring constantly. Slowly pour in the water and stir until the gravy thickens. Stir in the vegetables and add the chicken pieces.

Cover and simmer over low heat about 20 minutes or until the chicken is cooked through. Add salt and pepper to taste. Serve sauce over chicken and hot cooked rice, if desired.

# A Pecan By Any Other Name

My Aunt Betty was a true Southern Belle from Mobile, Alabama. I loved her lilting Southern drawl and the way she dropped the "r's" off the ends of her words.

She said "dolla" instead of dollar and "colla" instead of collar. As a child with little worldly experience, it seemed exotic to me.

I was puzzled, however, by the way she pronounced the word "pecan". Everyone I knew called these popular Southern nuts "pe-CAHNS". She said, "PEE-cans".

I presented this dilemma to my family's highest food authority—Granny O'Daniel.

"Why does Aunt Betty say, 'PEE-cans'," I asked her, "and we all say, 'pe-CAHNS'? How do I know which way is right?"

"Well, Glo-ry," my granny said, "here's the way I look at it: a pee can is what my mama kept under her bed at night."

I narrowed my eyes, trying to follow her logic. Since I was only six and had no experience with outdoor toilet facilities, I wasn't making the connection.

Granny shook her head in dismay. Modern-day young'uns sure didn't know much. "She kept it there so she didn't have to trek out to the outhouse during the middle of the night," she explained.

"Eeuwe!" I said. "She didn't have a bathroom?"

"Hardly anybody had bathrooms in this neck of the woods back then," she said. "That's why mama kept the can under her bed—a pee can. Does that help clear things up for you, child?"

"Yes, ma'am, it surely does. I'll never make that mistake!"

I'd never think of pecans in the same way again either, but that didn't mean I wouldn't enjoy eating them.

It doesn't matter how you pronounce it, there's nothing like the taste of my mama's pecan pie—all sweet and crunchy and warm from the oven.

It's like having your own little piece of heaven.

\*   \*   \*   \*   \*   \*   \*   \*

## Mama's Pecan Pie

3 large eggs, slightly beaten
1 cup corn syrup
1 cup granulated sugar
2 tablespoons butter or margarine, melted
1 teaspoon vanilla extract
1-1/2 cups chopped pecans
1 (9") pie shell

Preheat oven to 350°.

In a large bowl, stir together first 5 ingredients until well blended. Stir in nuts. Pour into pie shell. Bake 50-55 minutes or until knife inserted in center comes out clean.

# Five-Minute Chocolate Pecan Fudge

1 (14 oz.) can sweetened condensed milk
1 (12 oz.) pkg. semi-sweet chocolate chips
Dash of salt
1 teaspoon vanilla extract
1/2 cup chopped pecans

In a large saucepan, heat condensed milk and chocolate chips over medium-low heat, stirring constantly until chocolate chips are melted. Remove from heat.

Stir in salt, vanilla and pecans.

Pour into a buttered, 8" square pan. Or line pan with foil so you can lift out the fudge easily after it is set. Butter foil before adding fudge.

Let fudge cool. Cover and refrigerate until set.

Cut into squares. Store fudge in refrigerator until ready to serve.

Recipe makes 1-1/2 pounds of fudge.

# Spiced Pecans

1 egg white
1 teaspoon water
5 cups pecan halves
1/2 cup sugar
1/2 teaspoon ground cinnamon
1/4 teaspoon salt

Preheat oven to 225°.

In a mixing bowl, beat egg white and water with an electric mixer on high speed until foamy.

Stir in pecans until well coated.

In a small bowl, combine sugar, cinnamon and salt; sprinkle over pecans, stirring to coat thoroughly.

Spread pecans in single layer on a lightly greased baking sheet. Bake for 1 hour, stirring occasionally.

Leave on baking sheet until completely cooled. Store in an airtight container.

# German Chocolate Cake

2 cups sifted all-purpose flour
1 teaspoon baking soda
1/4 teaspoon salt
1 (4-oz.) pkg. German's Sweet Chocolate
1/2 cup boiling water
1 cup (2 sticks) butter or margarine
2 cups granulated sugar
4 egg yolks
1 teaspoon vanilla extract
1 cup buttermilk*
4 egg whites, stiffly beaten

Preheat oven to 350°. Line bottoms of three 9" layer pans with parchment or wax paper.

Melt chocolate in boiling water. Cool.

In a large bowl, cream butter and sugar until fluffy. Add yolks, one at a time, beating well after each. Blend in vanilla and chocolate.

In a separate bowl, sift flour with soda and salt; add alternately with buttermilk to chocolate mixture, beating after each addition until smooth.

Fold in beaten whites. Pour into cake pans and bake 30-35 minutes.

Cool cake layers on a wire rack. Frost the cake with coconut pecan frosting (recipe on page 26).


*If you don't have buttermilk, stir 1 tablespoon lemon juice or white vinegar into enough milk to equal 1 cup. Let stand for at least 5 minutes.

# Coconut Pecan Frosting

1-1/2 cups evaporated milk
1-1/2 cups granulated sugar
4 slightly beaten egg yolks
3/4 cup (1-1/2 sticks) butter or margarine
1-1/2 teaspoons vanilla extract
2 cups sweetened, flaked coconut
1-1/2 cups chopped pecans

In a large saucepan, cook and stir milk, sugar, egg yolks, butter and vanilla over medium heat until thickened and the color of caramel, about 12 minutes.

Remove from heat, stir in coconut and nuts and beat until spreading consistency.

Frost the top of cake and in between each cake layer. Leave sides of cake plain or frost if you prefer.

# Mind Your Manners

When I was a child, Southern mothers felt obliged to teach their children the importance of using good manners and showing respect for their elders.

"Always say, 'Yes, Ma'am' and 'No, Sir'," Mama told us.

I guess they equated age with wisdom, which, during my limited life experience, didn't always seem the case. My Aunt Joyce was older—and nuttier than a fruit cake.

She owned the only beauty shop in town and used her skills to change her hair color every month. Her wardrobe and makeup matched her personality—loud.

Since it was the mid-1950s and women's hairstyles were high maintenance, her business was brisk. But when she heard the funeral home was looking for someone to do their clients' hair, she jumped on it like a duck on a June bug.

"I don't think it's a good idea to bring dead people to the beauty parlor," Mama warned her. "It gives me the heebie jeebies just thinking about it," she said with a shiver.

"It will only be after closing time," Aunt Joyce argued. "Nobody will know." Or so she thought.

After her first delivery from the funeral home, Aunt Joyce had no sooner perched the dearly departed under the hair dryer when someone banged on the front door.

"Joyce, let me in," yelled Karen Mason, a long-time customer.

Aunt Joyce cracked the door open to peek out, and Karen pushed her way inside.

"I saw your lights were still on and wanted to drop off a plate of my favorite cookies to thank you for..."

Her gaze settled on the feet sticking out behind Aunt Joyce. She leaned to the side to offer a friendly, "Hey, there," to a fellow beauty client, but sucked in her breath. "That's S-S-Sarah," she screeched. "She's d-d-dead!"

Karen tossed the plate of cookies in the air and took off like greased lightning. The news spread fast about the cadaver cooties on the dryer chair at the beauty parlor, and Aunt Joyce's business took a nose dive.

But she didn't miss a beat. She stuck a "closed for remodeling" sign on the front door, repainted, refinished and re-named her shop and was open again in two shakes of a sheep's tail.

She was all smiles when my mama showed up for her next hair appointment. "I ran into Karen over at the A&P this morning," she said. "Bless her heart, her hair looked like the cat sucked it!"

"She still won't come back to the shop?" asked Mama.

"Don't that take the cake?" said Aunt Joyce. "And over something so silly. Dead women need to get their hair done, too. No self-respecting Southern lady wants to go to her grave on a bad hair day."

"God's truth," Mama said.

# Coconut Peanut Butter Bars

1 cup all-purpose flour
1/2 cup vegetable shortening
1/2 cup peanut butter
1/4 cup firmly packed brown sugar
1 cup granulated sugar
1 teaspoon vanilla extract
2 large eggs
1 teaspoon baking powder
1/4 teaspoon salt
1 can sweetened, flaked coconut

Preheat oven to 350°.

In a large bowl, cream together shortening, peanut butter and sugar until light and fluffy.

Add vanilla and eggs and beat well.

In a separate bowl, blend together flour, baking powder and salt. Add to creamed mixture, stirring just until blended. Stir in coconut.

Spread evenly in a greased 13" X 9" baking pan.

Bake about 25 minutes or until golden brown. Cool in pan and cut into bars to serve. Makes 36 bars.

# Chocolate Chip Meringue Cookies

2 egg whites
1/2 cup sugar
1/2 teaspoon vanilla extract
1/8 teaspoon salt
1 cup (6 ounces) semi-sweet chocolate chips
1/2 cup finely chopped pecans

Preheat oven to 325°. Beat egg whites and vanilla extract until soft peaks form. Gradually beat in sugar and salt until mixture is very stiff and glossy. Fold in chocolate chips and pecans. Drop by teaspoonfuls onto a cookie sheet lined with foil. Bake for 30 minutes or until golden. Cookies should be completely dry inside. Cool completely before removing from cookie sheet. Makes about 36.

# Sand Tarts

1 cup butter or margarine, softened
2 cups all-purpose flour
1/3 cup powdered sugar
1 teaspoon baking powder
1 cup chopped pecans
2 teaspoons vanilla extract
1 cup powdered sugar for rolling cookies

Preheat oven to 350°. In a large bowl, cream butter. Sift together flour, 1/3 cup powdered sugar and baking powder. Add gradually to creamed butter, beating until well blended. Stir in pecans and vanilla extract. Form dough into small balls. Place on ungreased cookie sheet. Bake for 10-12 minutes. While still warm, roll in remaining powdered sugar. Makes 3-4 dozen.

# Lemon Bars

Crust:
1/2 cup (1 stick) unsalted butter, softened
1/4 cup powdered sugar
1 cup all-purpose flour
1/8 teaspoon salt

Lemon Filling:
1 cup granulated sugar
2 large eggs
1/3 cup fresh lemon juice (approximately two large
     lemons)
1 tablespoon grated lemon zest
2 tablespoons all-purpose flour

Preheat oven to 350°. Grease an 8" X 8" baking pan.

To Make Crust: In a large bowl cream butter and sugar until light and fluffy, using an electric mixer.

Add flour and salt and beat until the dough just comes together. Press onto the bottom of prepared pan. Bake for about 20 minutes, or until lightly browned. Remove from oven and place on a wire rack to cool while you make the filling.

To Make Filling: In a large bowl, beat the sugar and eggs until smooth. Add the lemon juice and zest and stir to combine. Stir in the flour. Pour filling over the crust and bake for about 20 minutes, or until filling has set. Remove from oven and place on a wire rack to cool.

To serve: Cut into squares and dust with powdered sugar. These are best eaten the day they are made but can be covered and stored in the refrigerator for a day or two. Makes 16 bars.

# Aunt Joyce's Cherry Nut Loaf

1/2 cup butter or margarine
3/4 cup granulated sugar
2 large eggs
1 teaspoon vanilla extract
2 cups all-purpose flour
1 teaspoon baking soda
1/4 teaspoon salt
1 cup buttermilk*
1 cup chopped pecans
1 (10 oz.) jar maraschino cherries, drained and chopped

Preheat oven to 350°. Grease and flour a 9" X 5" loaf pan.

In a large bowl, cream together butter, sugar, eggs and vanilla.

In a separate bowl, blend together flour, baking soda and salt. Add flour mixture alternately with buttermilk, beating until well blended.

Stir in nuts and cherries. Pour into prepared loaf pan. Bake approximately 1 hour or until toothpick inserted into center comes out clean.

Cool in pan 10 minutes before removing. Cool loaf on wire rack.

*If you don't have buttermilk, stir 1 tablespoon lemon juice or white vinegar into enough milk to equal 1 cup. Let stand for at least 5 minutes.

# Exposed

When naming their children, Southern parents don't tack on middle names just to fill in the blank on a birth certificate. If your given name is Donna Lynn or Iva Nell or Jimmy Lee, then that's what everyone calls you.

And if your mama uses your first, middle and last names all together in one sentence, you'd better hide because you're in big trouble.

Since I was a curious child, and a tomboy to boot, I heard my full name screeched a lot. I caused my poor mama no end of grief with my shenanigans.

One day after school, when I was in the second grade, I dashed off with a neighborhood friend to play on the swing set in his backyard. I loved to climb up on the cross bars and hang upside down from my knees.

Normally this wouldn't cause a problem, except that, in the mid-1950s, girls weren't allowed to wear shorts or slacks to school—only dresses and skirts.

When Mama looked out the kitchen window and saw me flashing my underpants at God and everybody else, she flew into a tizzy.

I flinched when I heard her voice, pitched two octaves above middle "C", "Gloria Jean Owens!"

I didn't see her stomping across the yard in my direction since my dress was hanging down over my head, but I felt her yank me off the swing set and give me a swat on the bottom that lifted me clean off the ground.

I was still trying to figure out what I'd done wrong this time when she launched into her tirade about how proper young ladies should behave.

The world is a complicated place, especially to a seven-year-old. "I didn't mean to show my underwear, Mama," I cried. "I was just playing and forgot I was wearing a dress."

Mama sighed and shook her head. "I know, darlin'. You've just got to learn to pay more attention. Maybe you ought to stay inside a while and help me with the desserts for the bake sale tomorrow."

My eyes widened. "Can I lick the spoon?"

We spent the afternoon in Mama's tiny, overheated kitchen, filled with the sweet scent of sugar, cinnamon and vanilla. The counters were soon covered with cookies, cakes and pies.

The next morning, I was happy as a pup with two tails when I saw the school clothes Mama had laid out by my bed. She'd placed a pair of shorts right next to my dress. I reckon she wanted to make sure I was "covered"—just in case I got the urge to hang upside down on the monkey bars again.

# Snickerdoodles

1 cup unsalted butter, softened
1-1/2 cups granulated sugar
2 large eggs
1 teaspoon vanilla extract
2-3/4 cups all-purpose flour
2 teaspoons baking powder
1/2 teaspoon salt
1/3 cup granulated sugar
2 teaspoons ground cinnamon

In a large bowl, cream butter and 1-1/2 cups sugar together. Beat in eggs, one at a time. Add vanilla extract.

Sift together flour, baking powder and salt. Stir into butter mixture.

Chill dough at least one hour.

Preheat oven to 400°.

In a small bowl, combine 1/3 cup sugar and 2 teaspoons cinnamon.

Form dough into 1" balls and roll in cinnamon mixture.

Place 2" apart on ungreased baking sheet. Using the bottom of a glass, gently flatten each cookie to 1/2" thick. Bake for 8-10 minutes.

Makes about 6 dozen cookies.

# Chocolate Crinkle Cookies

1/2 cup vegetable oil
4 squares unsweetened baking chocolate, melted
2 cups granulated sugar
4 large eggs
2 teaspoons vanilla extract
1/2 teaspoon salt
2 cups all-purpose flour
2 teaspoons baking powder
1 cup powdered sugar

In a large bowl, mix oil, chocolate and sugar. Add eggs one at a time until well blended. Stir in vanilla.

Add salt, flour and baking powder. Stir until well blended.

Chill dough several hours.

Preheat oven to 350°.

Place powdered sugar in a small bowl. Roll dough into 1" balls. Coat each ball with powdered sugar.

Place 2" apart on greased cookie sheet. Bake 10-12 minutes. Cool cookies on wire racks.

# Sugar Cookies

1 cup vegetable shortening
1 cup granulated sugar
2 large eggs, slightly beaten
3 cups all-purpose flour
1/4 teaspoon salt
1/2 teaspoon baking soda
1/2 teaspoon baking powder
1 teaspoon vanilla extract

In a large bowl, cream together shortening and sugar. Beat in eggs. Sift dry ingredients together and mix into shortening mixture. Add vanilla. Chill dough for about 1 hour. Form dough into small balls and place about 1" apart on a greased cookie sheet. Press each ball with the bottom of a glass that has been dipped in flour. Sprinkle with sugar. Bake at 375° for about 7 minutes or until light brown.

You can also roll this dough out to about 1/4" thick and cut out cookies using cookie cutters in various shapes.

Let the baked cookies cool on a wire rack and then frost using the following recipe:

# Sugar Cookie Icing

Mix together 2 cups powdered sugar, 1 teaspoon vanilla extract and 3 tablespoons milk or cream, as needed to achieve spreading consistency. Tint icing with food coloring of your choice, if desired. Spread icing on cooled cookies.

# Banana Nut Bread

1-3/4 cups all-purpose flour
3/4 cup granulated sugar
1/2 cup chopped pecans
1 teaspoon baking powder
1/4 teaspoon baking soda
1/4 teaspoon salt
1 teaspoon ground cinnamon
2 large eggs, slightly beaten
1/2 cup butter, melted and cooled
3 large bananas, mashed (about 1-1/2 cups)
1 teaspoon vanilla extract

Preheat oven to 350°.

Grease and flour the bottom and sides of a 9" x 5" x 3" loaf pan.

In a large bowl, combine the flour, sugar, baking powder, baking soda, salt, cinnamon and nuts.

In a medium bowl combine bananas, eggs, butter and vanilla. Stir banana mixture into dry ingredients just until moistened.

Pour batter into prepared pan. Bake 55-60 minutes or until bread is golden brown and a toothpick inserted in the center comes out clean.

# Armed and Dangerous

When I was in second grade, I walked to school every weekday, toting my books and beloved Peter Pan lunchbox. I sashayed along at a pretty good clip, my long ponytail swishing side-to-side, keeping time with each step.

Gary, a boy from my class, liked to follow along behind me on my way to school. I knew he was sweet on me, so I didn't mind—as long as he kept a respectable distance.

One fateful day, however, he grabbed me and planted a kiss on my cheek. I was mad as an old wet hen and whacked him over the head with my metal lunchbox.

I was chompin' at the bit to get home from school that day and tell Mama what he'd done, so she could tell his mama, and Gary would get his hide tanned, for sure. Southern gentlemen were taught to mind their manners. What he did was just plain tacky.

I was thankful that I had my lunchbox to put him in his place, but it was never the same after the head-whacking incident. The top was bashed in, so it just wouldn't stay closed. Every day on my way to school, the dang thing fell open and my sandwich plopped out onto the sidewalk.

Mama tried putting a big rubber band around it, but the first time I tried to pull it off at lunchtime, it flew across the room and slapped my teacher right square in the back. She never did figure out who shot her with a rubber band, and I sure as heck wasn't going to tell.

But that afternoon, Principal Bailey sent home a memo to all parents saying that, under no circumstances were students allowed to bring rubber bands to school—they were dangerous weapons—especially to his staff.

Undaunted, Mama got the brilliant idea to tie one of my hair ribbons into a bow around my broken lunchbox.

I was thrilled. It was like carrying a birthday present to school every day—my lowly sandwich was elevated to party status.

In a matter of days, all the other second-grade girls had ribbons tied around their lunchboxes, too. It turned out to be the fashion statement of the year!

\*　\*　\*　\*　\*　\*　\*　\*

Note: You can use all these sandwich filling recipes for party sandwiches. After spreading the filling on the bread, trim away the crusts and cut each sandwich into four triangles.

# Aunt Bea's Tuna & Apple Salad

1 (6 oz.) can solid albacore tuna, drained and flaked
1 large hardboiled egg, chopped
1/4 cup chopped red apple
1/4 cup chopped celery
1/4 cup chopped pecans
1 teaspoon minced onion or 1/4 teaspoon onion
    powder
1/2 cup mayonnaise (or to taste)
1 teaspoon lemon juice

In a medium bowl, combine all ingredients. Cover and refrigerate until ready to serve. Use as a sandwich filling or serve on lettuce leaves.

# Traditional Egg Salad

4 large hardboiled eggs
3 tablespoons mayonnaise
2 teaspoons dill pickle relish (or sweet if you prefer)
1/2 teaspoon onion powder
1/2 teaspoon prepared yellow mustard
Salt and pepper to taste

Peel eggs and place in a medium bowl. Mash the eggs with a fork. Add mayonnaise, pickle relish, onion powder, mustard, salt and pepper; stir until well blended. Cover and refrigerate until ready to serve. Use as a sandwich filling.

# Southern Pimiento Cheese Spread

1 pound shredded Cheddar cheese
1 (4-oz.) jar diced pimentos
1/4 teaspoon garlic powder
1/2 teaspoon onion powder
Ground black pepper to taste
1/2 cup mayonnaise (or to taste)

In a medium bowl, mix all ingredients well. Cover and refrigerate until ready to serve. Use as a sandwich filling.


# Creamy Ham & Pineapple Spread

1 (8 oz.) package cream cheese, softened
1/2 cup ground, smoked, fully-cooked ham
1/2 cup crushed pineapple, drained
    (reserve some juice)

In a small bowl, blend together the cream cheese, ham and pineapple. Stir in a small amount of the reserved juice if needed for a more spreadable consistency. Cover and refrigerate until ready to serve. Use as a sandwich filling.

# Let the Good Times Roll

My family moved from Louisiana to a small town on the Texas Gulf Coast in 1957, when I was seven. Mama had relatives there and the booming job market reeled my daddy in, too.

I'll never forget the day I met my Aunt Fern. She was a vivacious Kentucky horse-lover who moved to Texas when she married Mama's cousin. They didn't have any kids for us to play with, but she had the most beautiful house I'd ever seen.

She loved to entertain friends and family with elaborate parties. Her annual Kentucky Derby shindig was the biggest ticket in town. My family didn't give a hoot about horse racing, but we were always up for partying.

In honor of the day, Aunt Fern served Mint Juleps and Kentucky (Bourbon) Derby Pie. As a nod to her new home state, she baked her famous Texas Tipsy Cake.

By the time the guests arrived, her cake wasn't the only thing that was tipsy. Aunt Fern liked to tipple while she baked.

But she was a gracious host and an excellent cook. The party room was festive with flowers, candles and sparkling lights. The buffet table groaned under the weight of delectable appetizers and irresistible desserts.

And she never forgot the young'uns—we squealed with delight over our giant chocolate brownie sundaes.

As the party wound down, Aunt Fern was just hitting her stride. One year, after downing a few Mint Juleps and sampling the tipsy cake and bourbon pie, she hopped up on the coffee table to entertain the guests with her favorite tap-dancing routines.

"Mama," I asked. "Is Aunt Fern three sheets to the wind?"

Mama giggled. "Yes, darlin', she surely is."

*  *  *  *  *  *  *  *

## Mint Juleps

2 cups sugar
2 cups water
Fresh mint leaves
Crushed ice
Bourbon Whiskey

In a large saucepan, mix sugar and water together. Bring to a boil and cook for five minutes to make the syrup. Let cool and place in a covered container with 10-12 fresh mint leaves. Refrigerate overnight.

To make one julep: Fill a glass (8 oz.) with crushed ice. Add one tablespoon mint syrup, 1 tablespoon water and two ounces of Bourbon Whiskey. Stir. Garnish with a sprig of fresh mint, if desired.

# Aunt Fern's Texas Tipsy Cake

Cake:
1 cup chopped pecans
1/2 cup water
1 (18-1/2 oz.) pkg. yellow cake mix
1 package vanilla pudding (4-serving size)
4 large eggs
1/2 cup vegetable oil
1/2 cup dark rum

Glaze:
1/4 lb. butter
1/4 cup water
1 cup granulated sugar
1/2 cup dark rum

To Make Cake:
Preheat oven to 325°. Grease and flour a 10-cup Bundt pan. Sprinkle chopped pecans in bottom of pan. In a large bowl, combine water, cake mix, pudding, eggs, oil and rum. Beat with an electric mixer until fluffy and well blended. Pour batter over the nuts in the pan. Bake 1 hour or until a toothpick inserted in center of cake comes out clean. Remove from pan and cool on a wire rack.

To Make Glaze:
In a medium saucepan, cook all glaze ingredients except rum over low heat for 5 minutes, stirring constantly. Remove from heat and let cool for 2 minutes. Stir in rum. Use an ice pick or knife to make holes in the cake. Slowly, drizzle glaze over the cake, allowing it to seep through the holes into the cake.

# Kentucky Derby Pie

4 large eggs
1/2 cup granulated sugar
1/4 cup brown sugar, firmly packed
1 cup light corn syrup
6 tablespoons butter or margarine, melted
3 tablespoons bourbon
1 tablespoon all-purpose flour
2 teaspoons vanilla extract
1 cup coarsely chopped pecans
1 cup semisweet chocolate chips
1 (9-inch) unbaked deep dish pie crust

Preheat oven to 350°.

Whisk together first 8 ingredients.

Stir in pecans and chocolate chips. Pour into pie crust. Place pie on a baking sheet.

Bake on lowest oven rack 55 minutes or until set. Cover edges of pie crust with strips of foil if needed to prevent over-browning.

Cool completely on wire rack before serving.

# Chocolate Rum Balls

1 cup finely crushed vanilla wafers
1 cup finely chopped pecans, toasted*
1-1/2 cups powdered sugar, divided
2 tablespoons unsweetened cocoa powder
2 tablespoons Rum or Bourbon
1-1/2 tablespoons light corn syrup

Combine vanilla wafer crumbs, pecans, cocoa and 1 cup of the powdered sugar.

In a measuring cup, blend the Rum and corn syrup; stir into the dry mixture until well blended.

Cover and refrigerate batter for an hour or more.

Sift about 1/2 cup of powdered sugar into a small bowl.

Shape small amounts of the dough into 1" balls then roll in the powdered sugar.

Store tightly covered in the refrigerator. Makes about 3 dozen.


*To toast the pecans, place in a dry skillet over medium-high heat. Stir constantly for several minutes until golden brown.

# Chocolate Kahlúa Brownies

1-1/2 cups all-purpose flour
1/2 teaspoon baking powder
1/2 teaspoon salt
2/3 cup butter or margarine
3 squares (1 oz. each) unsweetened baking chocolate
3 large eggs
2 cups granulated sugar
1/4 cup Kahlúa
3/4 cup chopped pecans

Preheat oven 350°. Grease a 9" square pan.

In a large bowl, combine flour with baking powder and salt.

In a small saucepan, melt butter with chocolate over low heat. Let cool slightly.

In a small bowl, beat eggs with sugar until well blended. Add to flour mixture. Stir in chocolate mixture and 1/4 cup Kahlúa. Mix well. Stir in nuts.

Pour batter into prepared pan. Bake 30 minutes or until top springs back when touched lightly in center, and edges begin to pull away from pan. Cool completely in pan and cut into squares.

# Making a Splash

My Granny O'Daniel loved to fish on Caddo Lake. She spent many leisurely hours sitting on an old quilt spread out on the bank, wearing a broad-brimmed straw hat, and catching catfish with her bamboo pole.

One summer, when my sisters and I came for visit, she took us along. At the ages of five, seven and nine, we soon tired of sitting and waiting for fish, so we spent our time looking for treasure on the bank and playing on a short wooden pier that jutted out into the water.

During a rousing game of tag, I accidentally stepped off the edge of the pier and landed head-over-tea-kettle in the water. Since none of us could swim, we were all in a panic—especially me! I bobbed up to the surface, coughing and splashing. My sisters froze in horror.

"Help!" screamed my older sister, Anna. "Gloria's gonna drown!"

Granny glanced over at me, shook her head in disbelieve and continued to fish.

When I went under for the second time, my younger sister, Charlotte, ran screaming down the pier, "Help, Granny, help!"

By the time I struggled to the surface again, Granny O'Daniel was standing, hands on hips, at the edge of the bank. "Stand up, child!" she yelled.

I snapped to attention and stood up straight as a board. I was standing in water barely up to my chest.

Not only was I soaked to the skin and coughing up water, I was mortified with embarrassment as I stomped toward the shore.

Granny figured she might as well give up on the fishing. After all that commotion, the fish had probably high-tailed it to Mississippi by now. She bundled me up in her old quilt and packed us off for home.

I never was inclined to go back to the lake after that summer, but the catfish sure was tasty. It was crispy and golden on the outside and warm and flaky on the inside. Just the way I like it!

\* \* \* \* \* \* \* \*

## Southern Fried Catfish

Rinse four catfish fillets with cold water.

Melt shortening in a large iron skillet. It should be about 1/2-inch deep.

In a shallow dish, combine 1/4 cup of flour and 1 cup of white cornmeal.

Season the fillets with salt and pepper then roll in the cornmeal mixture to coat well; gently shake off excess.

When the fat is hot but not smoking (about 375°), carefully lay the fillets in the skillet. Fry until crisp and golden brown on the bottom, about 4 minutes. Turn carefully and fry the other side. Remove and drain on paper towels.

# Fish Gravy

1/2 cup white cornmeal
1/2 cup chopped onion
1/2 cup grease strained from cooking catfish
2 cups water (or as needed for gravy)*
Salt and ground black pepper to taste

After cooking catfish, strain 1/2 cup oil into a measuring cup. Wipe out the skillet.

Pour strained oil back into the skillet. Stir in cornmeal and onions and cook over medium high heat until cornmeal is browned and onion is tender.

Stir in water a little at a time and continue cooking until gravy is thickened. Add more water as needed to make gravy the consistency you prefer. Gravy will thicken more as it cools.

Add salt and black pepper to taste. Serve with fried catfish.


*You can substitute milk for the water or half of the water if you prefer.

# Hush Puppies

2 cups white corn meal
1 tablespoon granulated sugar
2 teaspoons baking soda
1 teaspoon salt
1 tablespoon finely minced onion
1 large egg
1 cup buttermilk*
4 to 5 tablespoons cold water
Oil for frying

Stir corn meal, sugar, soda and salt together.

Place onion in a small bowl. Add egg and buttermilk and beat until frothy. Pour into cornmeal mixture and stir lightly to mix.

Add just enough water to form a dough that is thick enough for dropping. Dough should hold its shape in the spoon. Drop by tablespoonfuls into about 3" of hot oil (about 360°) for about 2 minutes, turning to keep all sides evenly browned.

Makes about 2 dozen.


*If you don't have buttermilk, stir 1 tablespoon lemon juice or white vinegar into enough milk to equal 1 cup. Let stand for at least 5 minutes.

# Creamy Coleslaw

8 cups coarsely shredded cabbage (about 1 head)
1/4 cup coarsely shredded carrot
2 tablespoons finely minced onion
1/3 cup granulated sugar
1/2 teaspoon salt
1/8 teaspoon ground black pepper
1/2 cup mayonnaise
1/4 cup milk
1/4 cup buttermilk
1-1/2 tablespoons white vinegar
2-1/2 tablespoons lemon juice

Mix together cabbage, carrots and onion in a large bowl.

In a small bowl, blend together remaining ingredients.

Pour over the cabbage mixture and mix until thoroughly coated.

Cover bowl and refrigerate for several hours or overnight before serving.

# Peach Cobbler

This dessert is quick and easy, and makes a fine ending to a tasty catfish dinner.

2 (16-ounce) cans sliced peaches, drained
1-1/2 tablespoons lemon juice
1/2 cup brown sugar, firmly packed
1/2 teaspoon ground cinnamon
3/4 cup self-rising flour
1/2 cup granulated sugar
1/2 teaspoon baking powder
Dash salt
3/4 cup milk
1/3 cup melted butter or margarine

Preheat oven to 350°.

Arrange peaches in a 2-quart baking dish. Drizzle with lemon juice. Sprinkle with brown sugar and cinnamon.

In a medium bowl, combine flour, granulated sugar, baking powder and salt. Stir in milk until smooth.

Pour batter over peaches. Drizzle melted butter over batter. Bake about 50 minutes or until batter is done.

Top each serving with vanilla ice cream, if desired.

# The Great Outdoors

Southerners are known for their slow speech and laid-back pace. We like to take our time. You won't find any "New York minutes" down here. Our "fifteen minutes of fame" take at least 30 minutes—maybe more. Even one-syllable words are often stretched into two. Instead of hour, we say "ow-wer". Instead of pan, we say "pa-yun".

As a child, I was blessed, or cursed as the case may be, with an over abundance of curiosity and determination to learn as much as possible—the sooner the better. Much to my family's dismay, my constant need for exploration often clashed with their desire for a more leisurely pace.

Many of my summer vacations were spent camping in Arkansas with a bunch of my aunts, uncles and cousins. We slept in tents at a wooded camp ground, floated on inner tubes in the chilly, spring-fed lake and cooked hearty meals outside on two-burner camping stoves.

One afternoon, my cousin, Donna Lynn, and I headed back to our campsite from the lake. We skipped along the main dirt path, with our inner tubes slung over our shoulders.

My curiosity got the better of me, and I veered off onto a narrow path leading down to a stand of tall trees.

"You can't go down they-er," said Donna Lynn, running after me. "You have to stay on the pa-uth."

"I want to climb one of those trees," I said.

"No!" she argued, grabbing my inner tube. "You'll get lost!"

"Let go!" I yelled.

"No!" she screeched, tugging harder.

I yanked the tube from her hands and we both fell backwards into a thick patch of weeds.

"Land sakes!" yelled my Aunt Dell. "You young'uns get out of that poison ivy!"

My cousin and I spent the rest of our vacation covered in calamine lotion, trying desperately not to scratch the itchy, red rash. But the cookout food surely was a comfort.

Eating "out-dough-wers" just seems to make good food taste even better.

\* \* \* \* \* \* \* \*

## S'Mores

We loved making s'mores on our family camping trips. My daddy would cut and trim a thin tree branch for each of the kids to use for roasting our marshmallows.

The real trick was getting the marshmallows close enough to the fire to melt them but not so close that they caught on fire and turned into charcoal briquettes.

We smashed the melted marshmallows between two graham crackers lined with Hershey's chocolate bars. They were gooey and scrumptious!

Mama followed up with a wet wash rag because a lot of our dessert ended up stuck to our fingers and faces. Yum!

# Skillet Potatoes

It's customary in the South to pour cream-style corn over each serving of these tasty potatoes.

4 – 5 large white potatoes, thinly sliced
1 large onion, peeled and thinly sliced
1/2 cup (1 stick) butter
Salt and ground black pepper to taste

Melt butter in a large skillet over medium heat. Stir in potatoes and onions. Sprinkle with salt and pepper.

Cook, turning occasionally until lightly browned. Cover and steam for about ten minutes, turning occasionally, until tender.

# Mashed Potato Pancakes

2 cups prepared mashed potatoes
1 large egg, beaten lightly
6 tablespoons all-purpose flour
2 tablespoons grated onion
Salt and ground black pepper to taste
2 tablespoons vegetable oil

In a large bowl, combine potatoes, egg, flour, onion salt and pepper. Mix until well blended.

In a large skillet, heat oil over medium-high heat. Drop large spoonfuls of potato mixture into hot oil, flattening with the back of the spoon to about 1/2-inch thick. Fry until golden brown, about 2 minutes on each side. Serve hot.

# Fried Okra

4 cups sliced okra (fresh or frozen)
1 cup white cornmeal
2 tablespoons all-purpose flour
1 large egg
1/2 teaspoon salt
1/4 teaspoon ground black pepper (or to taste)
Vegetable oil, enough to cover okra completely in frying pan

Heat oil in a large frying pan on medium heat.

Beat egg lightly in a large bowl and add okra. Stir to coat.

Combine cornmeal, flour, salt and pepper in a separate large bowl. Dredge okra in the cornmeal mixture, tossing well to coat.

Place one piece of okra in the hot oil to test the temperature. If the oil is not hot enough, increase heat slightly until one piece of okra sizzles when dropped in the oil.

Add all of the okra to the oil and cook, stirring frequently, until golden brown. Drain on paper towels.

# Salmon Patties

1 (16 oz.) can salmon
1 small onion, grated
1 tablespoon dried parsley flakes
Ground black pepper, to taste
2 large eggs, well beaten
1 to 1-1/2 cups fine dry bread crumbs
Vegetable oil for frying

Place salmon and liquid into a medium mixing bowl. Flake with a fork, removing bones and skin.

Mix in grated onion, parsley and pepper. Stir in beaten eggs. Add enough bread crumbs, about 1/2 to 3/4 cup, to make mixture thick enough to shape into 12 small patties.

Roll patties in 1/2 cup bread crumbs.

In a large skillet, pour just enough vegetable oil to cover the bottom. Heat over medium heat; add patties.

Fry patties slowly on one side until golden brown. Turn patties and fry until brown on the other side. Drain on paper towels.

# Scalded Cornbread

2 cups white cornmeal
1/2 cup self-rising flour
1/2 teaspoon salt
3 cups boiling water (you will use less)
Vegetable oil for frying

In a large bowl, mix cornmeal, flour and salt.

Pour in boiling water gradually, stirring until the cornmeal mixture is thick enough for shaping. Let cool slightly.

Form into 3" patties about 1/2" thick, using wet hands.

Into a large skillet, pour just enough vegetable oil to cover the bottom and heat over medium-high heat.

Place patties in pan and lower heat to medium. Cook patties about 5 minutes on each side or until golden brown. Drain on paper towels.

# When We All Get Together

My mama's family held their annual reunions every summer on her uncle's farm, about 20 miles from home.

As is the case with most Southern family reunions, these gatherings were all about hugging and eating.

"You're a sight for sore eyes!" they said. "Here, have some fried chicken."

Family members brought their favorite foods to share. The tables were crowded with traditional Southern dishes, and by the end of the day, we were all full as ticks.

When I was barely two years old, I insisted on making the journey with my grandparents in their 1936 Ford sedan. There was no such thing as a child seat during those days. I stood proudly on the back seat, enjoying the breeze blowing through the windows and taking in the scenery of the surrounding countryside.

My granny's contribution to the group's menu that year was her signature jelly cake, which she carefully placed on the back seat floorboard to keep it safe from my curious little fingers.

The car crawled along at a snail's pace over the bumpy dirt roads, through a string of tiny country towns. As my granddaddy approached the main intersection in Ida, a tractor barreled across the road from behind a general store.

"Stop!" yelled Granny.

He slammed on the brakes and we all lurched forward—some of us more than others. I found myself on the floor of the car, head-first in the jelly cake.

"Well, Glo-ry," Granny said, wiping the gummy mess off my face. "You're gonna be sweeter than ever now, sugar."

My trip had started off with a nasty turn, but it wasn't all bad. Even though I spent the rest of the day with a cloud of flies circling the sugary goo in my hair, I was the only one who got a taste of the jelly cake—except for Granny who had kissed the bump on my head to make it all better. Or so she said.

It was the beginning of my lifelong love affair with dessert.

\*   \*   \*   \*   \*   \*   \*   \*

## Traditional Southern Deviled Eggs

7 large eggs, hardboiled and peeled
1/4 cup mayonnaise
1-1/2 tablespoons sweet (or dill) pickle relish
1 teaspoon prepared mustard
Salt and ground black pepper to taste
Paprika (optional)

Cut eggs in half lengthwise. Remove yolks and place in a small bowl. Mash yolks with a fork and stir in mayonnaise, pickle relish and mustard. Add salt and pepper, to taste. Fill egg whites evenly with yolk mixture. Sprinkle with paprika, if desired. Store covered in refrigerator until ready to serve.

# Pineapple Glazed Ham

1 (4 to 5 pound) fully cooked, boneless ham
1 (8 oz.) can pineapple slices
1/3 cup honey
1 tablespoon ground mustard
Dash ground cloves

Preheat oven to 325°. Place ham on rack in shallow baking pan and bake for 1 hour or to 120° F. on meat thermometer.

Drain pineapple; reserve liquid. Combine reserved liquid, honey, mustard and cloves; mix well.

Score top of ham in a diamond pattern, if desired, and arrange pineapple slices on top. Generously brush honey mixture over entire surface.

Bake about 30 to 45 minutes longer or to 140° F.; baste every 10 minutes.

Let stand 10 to 15 minutes before slicing.

Makes 12 to 16 servings.

# Baked Beans

4 slices of smoked bacon
1/4 cup chopped onion
2 (16-ounce) cans pork 'n beans, undrained
1/4 cup tomato ketchup
2 tablespoons brown sugar, firmly packed
1 teaspoon prepared mustard

In a large skillet, cook bacon until crisp; drain on paper towels and crumble.

Drain most of the fat from pan and sauté onion until tender.

Stir in bacon and remaining ingredients until well blended.

Pour mixture into a greased, shallow baking dish and bake in a preheated 350° oven for 35-40 minutes, until beans are brown and bubbly.

# Potato Salad

6 cups cooked, peeled and cubed red potatoes
    (about 6 medium)
3 hardboiled eggs, diced
1/2 cup finely chopped celery
1/4 cup dill pickle relish
2 tablespoons finely minced onion (or to taste)
3/4 cup mayonnaise (or 1/2 cup mayonnaise & 1/4
    cup sour cream)
1 teaspoon prepared mustard
1/2 teaspoon salt (or to taste)
Dash of ground black pepper

Blend all ingredients in a large bowl. Add more mayonnaise if needed. Cover and chill several hours. Stir again before serving.

# Turnip Greens

4 to 4-1/2 pounds turnip greens
1 pound salt pork, rinsed and diced
1-1/2 cups water
1 cup finely chopped onion
Salt and ground black pepper to taste
1 teaspoon sugar, optional
Dash of crushed red pepper, optional

Remove tough stems from greens. Wash thoroughly and drain well. Cook salt pork in a large pot or Dutch oven over medium heat until crisp and brown. Add turnip greens, water, onion, salt, pepper, sugar and crushed red pepper. Bring to a boil. Reduce heat, cover, and simmer 40 to 45 minutes or until greens are tender. Serve with vinegar or pepper sauce and cornbread.

# Jelly Cake

1 cup butter or margarine, softened
2 cups granulated sugar
4 large eggs
3 cups self-rising flour
1 cup whole milk
1 teaspoon vanilla extract
2 cups fruit jelly of your choice (Granny O'Daniel
    used her homemade mayhaw jelly)

Preheat the oven to 350°.

Grease and flour a 9x13 inch pan or 3 (8") pans.

In a large bowl, cream together butter and sugar until light and fluffy. Beat in eggs one at a time, mixing well after each.

Stir in flour and milk, alternately. Mix in vanilla.

Pour batter into prepared pan(s).

Bake 9" X 13" cake for 35 to 40 minutes or layers for 25 to 30 minutes, or until center springs back when pressed lightly.

Poke holes in the cake with a fork or knife and spread with jelly while it is warm, but not hot, so the jelly will soak into the cake.

Note: You can use a yellow cake mix for the cake if you prefer.

# Bless Your Heart

Southern women have concocted the most ingenious method for insulting someone, while seeming quite caring and innocent. They simply insert the words "bless her heart" before each insult.

"Bless her heart, she's so ugly her mama had to tie pork chops to her ears just to get the dawg to play with her."

"Poor thing," we all reply. "What a shame."

After my family moved from Louisiana to Texas in 1957, our closest relatives were my Aunt Bea and Uncle Russell, who lived about 30 minutes away in Houston. Aunt Bea was non-stop motion and chatter; Uncle Russell was slower than molasses in January.

Since most of our family still lived far away in Louisiana, we visited Aunt Bea often for trips to the zoo, picnics in the park and the annual Thanksgiving Day Parade.

Unfortunately, we spent a lot of time waiting for Uncle Russell. Everyone piled into cars, ready to hit the road, while he made his usual rounds, checking that all the lights were off, the windows were locked and the pilot light was still burning in the water heater. It just wouldn't do to have the house explode while we were picnicking in the park.

After too many of these delays, we finally started leaving him behind. By the time we got back, he was ready to go. But the parade had passed him by.

One Thanksgiving, as the ladies flitted around preparing the day's fare, my aunt gave him a head's up. "Russell, go ahead a get washed up for dinner, darlin'."

Uncle Russell sat like a bump on a log, reading the newspaper in his favorite chair.

Soon the women put the final touches on the meal and carted it off to the table.

"Russell," said Aunt Bea. "It's time to eat. Come on to the table."

There was still no sign of motion from his chair. But the rest of the clan took their places around the table, impatiently waiting to pounce on our favorite holiday fixin's.

"Russell!" she yelled. "Get over here now. We're waitin' on you!"

He calmly folded the newspaper, placed it on his desk, turned off the light and began a slow shuffle in our direction.

"Bless his heart," said Aunt Bea. "He couldn't get anywhere on time if he was running out in front of a buffalo stampede."

She glanced around the table at our anxious faces and bowed her head. "Thank you Lord for the food we're about to receive. Amen."

"Amen!" we said. And we all dug in!

# Cornbread Dressing

3 cups crumbled cornbread
3 cups day-old bread cubes
2 tablespoons crumbled dried sage
2 teaspoons poultry seasoning (or to taste)
Salt and ground black pepper to taste
1 cup chopped celery
1/2 cup chopped onion
1/2 cup butter or margarine
2 large eggs, slightly beaten
3-4 cups chicken or turkey broth

Preheat oven to 350°. Grease a shallow 2-quart baking dish.

In a large skillet over medium heat, melt the butter and sauté celery and onion until tender.

In a large bowl, combine celery, onions, crumbled corn bread, bread cubes, eggs, chicken broth, sage, poultry seasoning, salt and pepper. Mix well. Dressing should be very moist, about the consistency of oatmeal.

Pour into prepared dish and bake for 30-35 minutes or until brown on top and set in the middle.

# Cornbread Dressing Gravy

1 can condensed chicken broth
1 cup water
1-1/2 cups cornbread dressing batter
   (remove before baking)
6 hardboiled eggs, chopped
1/2 cup finely chopped, cooked turkey meat
Optional: you can add the chopped, cooked giblets
   from the turkey if you like the taste
Salt and ground black pepper to taste

In a large saucepan, blend together chicken broth and water. Bring to a boil. Stir in remaining ingredients and cook over medium heat, stirring occasionally until slightly thickened. Serve over cooked cornbread dressing.

# Holiday Fruit Salad

2 cups apples, diced
1 cup green seedless grapes, cut in half
1/2 cup canned Mandarin orange sections, drained
1 cup miniature marshmallows
1/2 cup chopped pecans
2 teaspoons lemon juice
1 cup whipped cream
2 tablespoons granulated sugar (or to taste)

In a large bowl, toss apples with lemon juice. Mix in grapes, oranges, marshmallows and nuts. In a separate bowl, combine sugar and whipped cream. Mix thoroughly. Gently stir into fruit mixture. Serve immediately or cover and chill.

# Sweet Potato Casserole

**Casserole Ingredients:**
3 cups cooked, mashed sweet potatoes (or use canned)
1/2 cup granulated sugar
1/2 teaspoon salt
1/2 teaspoon ground cinnamon
2 eggs, slightly beaten
1/3 cup butter or margarine, softened
1/2 cup milk
1 teaspoon vanilla extract

**Topping Ingredients:**
1 cup brown sugar, packed
1 cup chopped pecans
1/3 cup all-purpose flour
1/3 cup butter or margarine, melted

Preheat oven to 350°.

In a large bowl, mix together all casserole ingredients until well blended.

Pour into a shallow, greased 1-1/2 quart baking dish.

In a medium bowl, mix together all the topping ingredients. Sprinkle on top of sweet potato mixture.

Bake for 30-35 minutes.

# Pumpkin Nut Bread

1-3/4 cups self-rising flour
1-1/2 cups granulated sugar
1/2 teaspoon ground cinnamon
1/4 teaspoon ground nutmeg (optional)
2 eggs, slightly beaten
1/2 cup vegetable oil
1 cup canned pumpkin purée
1/2 cup chopped pecans

Preheat oven to 325°. Lightly grease and flour a 9" X 5" loaf pan.

In a large bowl, combine flour, sugar, cinnamon and nutmeg.

In a separate bowl, combine eggs, oil and pumpkin. Add to flour mixture and stir until well blended. Stir in nuts.

Pour into prepared loaf pan and bake for about 1 hour and 10 minutes or until toothpick inserted into center comes out clean.

Let cool in pan on a wire rack for 10 minutes. Turn out onto rack to cool completely.

# Southern Hospitality

Southerners are known for being friendly. We do our best to make strangers feel welcome, no matter where they're from. Southern women are especially gracious. They call everybody by their first names—sugar, darlin' and honey.

My mama's sister, Aunt Trudy, was particularly fond of "hunnee". She was a master at one-word-communication, simply by changing her facial expressions and the tone of her voice.

"Hunnee" with a grimace meant, "No self-respecting Southern woman would be caught dead in that outfit!"

"Hunnie!" with raised eyebrows meant, "Don't even think about cleaning that smelly catfish in my kitchen sink!"

"Hunny" with a pathetic smile meant, "You're so ignert we couldn't find your little pea brain if we put it under a microscope."

The scary part was that everyone understood completely—no extra words required. Only on rare occasions did she use more than one word; like the time my family was invited for dinner when I was five.

There were twelve of us in all—my family of five, her family of six and my Granny O'Daniel. Since we couldn't all fit around the small dining room table, the men hauled in a large piece of plywood to place on top.

The ladies covered it with tablecloths and a mountain of food. We had meatloaf, potatoes, salads, cream-style corn, black-eyed peas and cornbread, plus an assortment of condiments and relishes—to be followed by the desserts waiting in the kitchen.

We all gathered around to find our places.

"Hop up on that bench," Mama told me, "and scoot over to make room for the rest of the young'uns."

I did as I was told and leaned both hands on the table top for leverage to scoot my bottom down the bench. But the board offered no resistance. Instead, it tipped over into my lap and all the food slid down on top of me.

Everyone stared in open-mouthed horror—except for Aunt Trudy.

"Gosh dang nabbit!" she cried.

The open-mouth stares turned from me to her. Granny O'Daniel was the first to find her voice.

"Sugar!" she said in her most reprimanding voice, meaning, "Proper ladies never, ever swear!"

Granny transferred her gaze to me, sighed and shook her head in dismay. "Darlin'," she said, meaning, "In all my born days I've never encountered such an accident-prone child."

I shrugged and swiped at the cream-style corn running down the side of my face. A truer word was never spoken!

# Aunt Trudy's Meatloaf

2 pounds lean ground beef
1 envelope dry onion soup mix
1/2 cup plain dry bread crumbs
1 large egg, slightly beaten
1 (8 oz.) can tomato sauce

Preheat oven to 350°. Lightly grease a 9" X 5" X 3" loaf pan.

In a large bowl, mix ground beef, soup mix, bread crumbs, egg and 1/2 cup of the tomato sauce until well blended.

Pack into loaf pan and bake, uncovered, for 1 hour. Drain fat.

Pour remaining tomato sauce over the top and cook for another 15 minutes or until done.

# Scalloped Potatoes

2 pounds (about 6 medium) potatoes, peeled and
thinly sliced
3 tablespoons butter or margarine
1/4 cup chopped onion
3 tablespoons all-purpose flour
1 teaspoon salt
1/4 teaspoon ground black pepper
1 (12 oz.) can evaporated milk
1 cup water
1/3 cup grated Parmesan cheese

Place potatoes in a large saucepan and cover with
water; bring to a boil. Cook over medium high heat
about 5 minutes; drain. Set aside.

Preheat oven to 350°. Grease an 11" x 7" baking dish.

In a medium saucepan, heat butter over medium heat.
Add onion and cook 2 to 3 minutes or until
tender. Stir in flour, salt and pepper. Gradually stir in
evaporated milk and water. Cook until mixture comes
to a boil, stirring constantly. Remove from heat.

Arrange potatoes in the prepared baking dish; pour
milk mixture over potatoes. Sprinkle with cheese. Bake
25 to 30 minutes or until potatoes are tender and
cheese is light golden brown.

# English Pea Salad

1 (10 oz.) package frozen English peas, thawed and
  drained
1/2 cup Cheddar cheese, cut into 1/4" cubes
1/2 cup chopped celery
1/2 cup chopped sweet red pepper or pimiento
1/4 cup finely chopped sweet pickles
2 tablespoons finely chopped green onion
2 hard boiled eggs, chopped
1/2 cup mayonnaise (or to taste)
Salt and ground black pepper to taste

Combine first seven ingredients.

Toss lightly with mayonnaise. Add salt and pepper to
taste.

Refrigerate several hours before serving.

# Banana Pudding

3/4 cup sugar
1/3 cup all-purpose flour
Dash of salt
2 eggs
2 cups milk
1 teaspoon vanilla
Box of vanilla wafers
5 or 6 ripe bananas, sliced (about 4 cups)

In a saucepan, blend sugar, flour and salt. Stir in eggs and milk. Cook over medium heat, stirring constantly until thickened. Remove from heat and stir in vanilla.

Spread 1/2 cup of custard into bottom of a 1-1/2 quart casserole dish.

Place a layer of vanilla wafers over custard.

Top with a generous layer of bananas. Pour about 2/3 cup of custard over the bananas.

Repeat with two more layers of vanilla wafers, bananas and custard.

Crush about 1/2 cup of wafers and sprinkle over the final layer of custard. Serve pudding warm or cold.

Optional: top each serving with sweetened whipped cream if you like.

# The National Dish of Texas

When my family moved from northern Louisiana to the Gulf Coast of Texas during the late 1950s, we discovered a wealth of new foods, from Tex-Mex to seafood. Mama was overwhelmed with all the possibilities, as friends and relatives shared their favorite recipes.

One evening, our neighbor invited us to dinner. "I'm serving 'the National Dish of Texas'," Myra said. "Come hungry and don't be late."

Anticipation was high as we scrambled next door at the appointed hour. Myra placed a huge platter on the table in front of us. "Chicken fried steak," she said, beaming with pride.

We each took a portion of meat, served with mashed potatoes, gravy and green beans, and dug in.

"It's delicious," Mama said. "What cut of beef is this?"

"Round steak," replied Myra.

"But how did you get it so tender?" asked Mama.

Myra's eyes sparkled with delight. "Come and see."

Mama followed her into the kitchen where Myra pulled a heavy metal hammer from a drawer, gazing upon it in awe. "It's a meat mallet," she whispered.

It was a frightening-looking tool, with sharp metal teeth on one side.

"How do you use it?" Mama asked.

Myra smiled. "You place the steak on the counter and hit it as hard as you can with these spikes." Bam! Bam! Bam! She demonstrated, beating the bejeezus out of a potholder on the counter.

Now Mama was smiling, too. She couldn't wait to get to the store the next day and buy her very own meat mallet.

I never understood her fascination with the evil-looking device. I didn't want to get near it. But Mama seemed to be transformed whenever she beat the living daylights out of that steak—humming and smiling the whole time. I have to admit, that chicken fried steak was melt-in-your mouth tender.

Now that I look back on it, I realize it was a 1950s version of housewife stress relief. Many years later, when I became a housewife, I never had any desire to own one of those hideous tools. I let the butcher take care of the tenderizing.

As for the housewife stress relief, our generation did girls' night out for nachos and margaritas—much more civilized in my opinion.

\*   \*   \*   \*   \*   \*   \*   \*

## Southern Green Beans

1-1/2 to 2 lbs. fresh green beans
2 slices smoked bacon
1 small onion, quartered
Salt and ground black pepper to taste

Remove the strings from the green beans and break into 1-inch pieces. Place in a large saucepan and cover with water. Add bacon and onion. Season with salt and pepper. Bring to a boil and reduce the heat. Cook on low until the beans are very tender, about 1 hour. Add more water if needed during cooking.

# Chicken Fried Steak with Cream Gravy

2 pounds round steak cut into serving size pieces and
    pounded to 1/4-inch thick with a kitchen mallet
1 cup all-purpose flour
Salt and ground black pepper
2 eggs, beaten with 2 tablespoons milk
Vegetable oil for frying

**Gravy:**
3 tablespoons vegetable oil (pan drippings after frying
    steak)
3 tablespoons flour
1 cup milk
1/2 cup chicken broth (or 1 teaspoon chicken bouillon
    granules dissolved in 1/2 cup water)
Salt and ground black pepper to taste

**To Make the Steaks:** Season flour with salt and
pepper. Dredge steaks in flour. Dip steaks in egg
mixture and dredge in flour again.

Heat about 1/4-inch of oil in a large skillet over
medium heat. Add steaks and cook 3-4 minutes per
side or until done. Keep warm while preparing gravy.

**To Make the Gravy:** Pour off all but about 3
tablespoons oil from skillet. Add about 3 tablespoons
flour to the pan drippings. (If you don't have quite
enough drippings, add a little more oil.)

Cook and stir flour over medium heat until lightly
browned. Add milk and broth. Continue to stir while
bringing to a boil. Reduce heat and cook about 5
minutes or until thickened. Add a little water if gravy
is too thick. Add salt and pepper to taste. Serve over
steaks.

# Texas Sheath Cake

Cake:
1 cup (2 sticks) butter
4 tablespoons unsweetened cocoa powder
1 cup water
2 cups all-purpose flour
2 cups granulated sugar
1 teaspoon baking soda
1/2 cup buttermilk*
2 large eggs, slightly beaten
1 teaspoon vanilla extract

Frosting:
1/2 cup (1 stick) butter or margarine
6 tablespoons milk
4 tablespoons unsweetened cocoa powder
1 (1 lb.) box powdered sugar
1 cup finely chopped pecans
1 teaspoon vanilla extract

**To Prepare Cake:** Preheat oven to 400°. Grease a 10 X 15-inch jelly roll pan. In a large bowl, blend together flour and sugar. In a saucepan, heat butter, cocoa and water until mixture comes to a boil. Remove from heat and stir into flour mixture. In a small bowl blend together buttermilk, eggs, baking soda and vanilla. Stir into flour mixture. Pour into prepared pan. Bake 20 minutes or until done. Frost cake while still hot.

**To Prepare Frosting:** In a large saucepan, heat butter, cocoa, and milk until boiling. Remove from heat and stir in powdered sugar, nuts and vanilla. Spread on top of warm cake.

*If you don't have buttermilk, stir 1/2 tablespoon lemon juice or white vinegar into enough milk to make 1/2 cup. Let stand for at least 5 minutes.

# Crab Wranglers

My family moved to a small town on the Texas Gulf Coast, about fifteen miles north of Galveston, in 1957. There, we discovered seafood—shrimp, crabs, oysters and more. Mama was in a tizzy, trying first one tasty recipe after another. Never having experienced seafood before, we couldn't believe our good fortune! We'd landed in seafood heaven.

My two sisters and I, ages five, seven and nine, soon discovered a small inlet on Galveston Bay within walking distance from our house. And, best of all, there were crabs in the shallow water underneath a short wooden pier.

One hot summer afternoon, we promised Mama we'd collect some crabs for dinner. The three of us set off down the dusty dirt road, heading for the bay. My older sister, Anna, swung the long-handled crab net over her shoulder, and I carried a large plastic bucket holding string and two chicken necks for bait. Charlotte, my younger sister, skipped along ahead of us, picking wildflowers and chasing horned toads on the side of the road.

We scurried out onto the pier, tied each chicken neck to the end of a string, dropped them into the water and tied the other ends of the string around one of the posts on the pier. Then we waited and watched for tiny bubbles to float to the surface, alerting us that a crab was nibbling on our bait.

"I see bubbles!" said Charlotte.

Anna grabbed the net. "Pull him up real slow so you don't scare him off."

Charlotte slowly raised the crab, "I see him! I see him!" she said, jerking the crab out of the water. The frightened critter let go and plopped back into the bay.

"You're supposed to let me get the net under him before you lift him out of the water!" said Anna.

Charlotte dropped the bait back into the water and plunked down onto the pier. And we all waited some more, sweating under the hot July sun.

"Here's another one," I said. "Get ready, Anna." I slowly inched the crab up to the surface so Anna could scoop him out of the water.

"You got him!" yelled Charlotte. "Put him in the bucket."

Anna flipped the net over the bucket, but the crab held tight. "He won't let go!"

"Give it a hard shake," I said. "Knock him loose!"

Anna thumped the net down hard on the edge of the bucket. The crab fell in, the bucket tipped over and the crab scooted across the pier straight for Charlotte's toes.

She squealed and danced around like a jumping bean, her pink flip flops slapping on the wooden planks.

The crab lunged and grabbed the edge of her shoe with his pincer, barely missing her little toe. Charlotte let out a piercing scream.

"Kick it off!" I yelled.

She squealed again and gave her foot a sharp kick. The crab sailed off into the water, still hanging on to Charlotte's shoe. He sank to the bottom of the bay and the shoe floated out to sea.

Charlotte was mad as a wet hen. "I'm going home!"

"But we didn't catch any crabs yet," I argued.

"I don't care. I'm leaving," she said, stomping down the pier on one shoe.

We snatched up our crabbing gear and headed for home. I reckon Mama hadn't put too much stock in our crab-wrangling abilities. She had dinner on the table by the time we walked through the door.

There was a huge platter piled high with golden fried shrimp, and baked potatoes and coleslaw on the side.

We were starving and plumb tuckered out. A hard day of crabbing sure does work up an appetite. Of course, we thanked our lucky stars we didn't need to catch any before we could eat.

# Golden Fried Shrimp

1-1/2 to 2 lbs. medium shrimp, shelled and deveined
2 large eggs
Wondra Quick Mix Flour*
Salt and ground black pepper to taste
Vegetable oil for frying

Pour about 2" vegetable oil into a large, deep skillet. Heat oil to about 375°.

Beat eggs in a small bowl.

Place flour in a separate small bowl and season with salt and pepper.

Dredge shrimp in flour mixture to coat. Shake off excess flour and dip into beaten eggs. Dredge again in flour and place in hot oil, a few at a time. Don't overcrowd the pan or the oil temperature will drop too low.

Cook shrimp about 1-2 minutes on each side or until golden brown and opaque inside. Don't overcook. Remove to paper towels to drain and keep warm in a low oven until all shrimp are cooked.

*Mama always used Wondra Flour to coat fried shrimp. It is made by General Mills. If you can't find it, use all-purpose flour instead. After coating the shrimp with flour and dipping in beaten eggs, you can then dredge them with plain bread crumbs if you prefer, for a crunchier coating.

# Shrimp-Stuffed Baked Potatoes

4 large Idaho potatoes, baked
5 tablespoons butter, divided
2 cups grated Cheddar cheese (reserve 1/4 cup for
   topping)
1 cup sour cream
2 tablespoons minced green onion tops or chives
Salt and pepper to taste
1 pound medium size shrimp, peeled and deveined
Paprika (optional)

Preheat oven to 350°.

Cook shrimp in a large skillet in 1 tablespoon of the butter over medium high heat until pink (about 3-4 minutes). Drain and set aside.

Slice each potato in half lengthwise. Gently scoop out the warm potato, leaving a 1/4" shell. Place potato pulp in a large bowl with remaining butter, sour cream, green onion, salt and pepper. Beat with electric mixer until fluffy.

Fold shrimp and cheese into potatoes. Fill potato shells with the mixture. Top each potato with 1 tablespoon reserved grated cheese and sprinkle lightly with paprika.

Place potatoes on a baking sheet and bake for 20 to 25 minutes, until heated through and lightly browned.

# Seafood Gumbo

1 lb. medium shrimp, peeled and deveined
1/2 lb. crabmeat
1/2 lb. fish filets, diced
1/3 cup all-purpose flour
1/3 cup vegetable oil
1-1/2 cups chopped onion
1 cup chopped bell pepper
1/2 cup chopped celery
3 cloves garlic, minced (or 1/2 teaspoon garlic powder)
2-1/2 cups chicken broth
1 (14-1/2 oz.) can diced tomatoes
2 cups sliced fresh or frozen okra (sauté before adding
    to gumbo, if you prefer)
1/2 teaspoon dried thyme leaves
2 bay leaves
Salt and ground black pepper to taste (or red pepper)
1 tablespoon Gumbo File powder
Hot cooked rice

Thaw shrimp, crab and fish if frozen.

Blend oil and flour in a 4-quart saucepan and cook over medium heat, stirring constantly until dark brown. Add onion, green pepper, celery and garlic. Sauté until vegetables are tender.

Add chicken broth, tomatoes, okra, bay leaves, thyme, salt and pepper. Cover and simmer 30 minutes, stirring occasionally. Add seafood. Simmer 8 to 10 minutes or until done.

Remove bay leaves. Stir in file powder. Serve over hot cooked rice.

# This Place is For the Birds

Since the South is "blessed" with long, hot summers, we grow fruit and vegetables practically all year long. And, bless our little pea-pickin' hearts, that means we're picking them pert near all year long, too.

My family went berry-picking in the spring for ripe red strawberries to make strawberry shortcake, and plump, sweet blackberries for blackberry cobbler. In the summer, we headed to the orchards for peaches and plums to bake pies and put up jars of jelly.

Mama kept a small vegetable garden out behind our house where she planted green onions, radishes, bell peppers and her prized tomatoes.

It was those tomato plants, however, that kept her tail feathers ruffled. No amount of weeding, watering and fertilizing could keep the pesky birds from eating her tomatoes.

As soon as they showed the slightest tinge of pink, those birds swooped down and devoured them. She tried scarecrows, fake owls, and even hung shiny tin pie pans from strings to scare them off, but nothing worked.

After a couple years of battling the birds, she gave up the tug of war over ripe tomatoes and decided to beat those birds to the punch—she'd pick them while they were still green. Those birds couldn't outsmart her!

It was a tad unconventional, but not a total loss. We ate fried green tomatoes, green tomato relish, and even green tomato cake.

Granny O'Daniel took pitty on us, and every now and then donated a basket of ripe, red tomatoes from her garden. Those birds didn't dare mess with the likes of her tomato patch.

I reckon that had something to do with her sixteen-pound guard cat, Rufus, who'd carved out a cozy home underneath her back porch in exchange for hunting privileges. To show her appreciation for a job well-done, Granny sprinkled a few catnip plants among the rows of vegetables. It was a match made in gardener's heaven!

*   *   *   *   *   *   *   *

## Southern Blackberry Cobbler

5 cups fresh (or frozen) blackberries
3/4 cups granulated sugar
1 tablespoon cornstarch
1/8 teaspoon salt
2 tablespoons butter or margarine
Pastry for 9" pie
1 tablespoon milk
1 tablespoon granulated sugar

Place blackberries in a 9" square baking dish. Combine 3/4 cup sugar, cornstarch and salt, mixing well. Sprinkle over blackberries. Dot with butter. Roll pastry out on a lightly floured surface to a 9" square. Place pastry on top of blackberries; trim edges and seal. Make several slits in the top to allow steam to escape. Brush pastry with milk; sprinkle with 1 tablespoon sugar. Bake at 425° for 30-35 minutes or until crust is golden brown and blackberries are bubbling.

# Fried Green Tomatoes

4 to 6 green tomatoes, sliced 1/4-inch thick
Salt and ground black pepper
All-purpose flour for dusting
2 eggs, beaten
Cornmeal for coating
Bacon grease or vegetable oil for frying

Sprinkle tomato slices with salt and pepper.

Dust lightly with flour.

Dip slices in beaten egg, letting excess drip off, then coat well with cornmeal.

Fry in hot grease or vegetable oil, just enough to cover the bottom of the pan, until golden brown, turning gently (about 3 minutes each side).

Keep warm in a low 200° to 250° oven if frying in batches.

# Green Tomato Cake

2-1/4 cups granulated sugar
1 cup vegetable oil
3 eggs
2 teaspoons vanilla
3 cups all-purpose flour
1/2 teaspoon salt
1 teaspoon baking powder
2 teaspoons ground cinnamon
1/2 teaspoon ground nutmeg
1 cup chopped pecans
3 cups diced green tomatoes

Preheat oven to 350°.

In mixing bowl, beat sugar, vegetable oil, eggs and vanilla until smooth and creamy.

Sift together flour, salt, baking powder, cinnamon and nutmeg; slowly beat into egg mixture. Blend well.

Stir in pecans and tomatoes.

Pour into greased 9" X 13" pan. Bake for one hour, or until a toothpick inserted in center comes out clean. Let cool completely in pan. Cut into squares to serve.

# Please Pass the Sugar

We Southerners surely do like our sweets. And I'm not just talking about dessert. When the temperature outside begins to creep up towards broil, there's nothing better than a tall glass of iced tea—the sweeter the better.

Sweet Iced Tea is a long-standing Southern tradition. To make it, we start by boiling black tea leaves in water for the maximum concentrated flavor, then strain the hot brew into a big pitcher and add sugar and more water.

It's a well-known chemical phenomenon that the hotter the water, the more sugar you can dissolve in it. Like I said, we like it sweet, so just keep stirring in the sugar. When the tea is just a bitty bit thinner than maple syrup, it's ready.

Pour it into a tall glass filled with ice and drop in a wedge of lemon. Don't use one of those wimpy lemon slices—it's got to be a wedge, so you can squeeze out all the juice and throw the whole thing into your tea. And never mind about those pesky seeds. After all, teeth aren't just for eating—they come in handy for straining, too.

Caffeine and sugar is a potent combination. Poured over ice and served up chilled, it makes the perfect thirst quencher for a sizzling hot day.

But tea isn't the only beverage we like sweet. How about a sweet and tangy lemonade or spicy mint julep? Mighty satisfying!

Down here in the South, our sugar cravings start early. From the time my two sisters and I were toddlers, we hated milk. It was bland and boring.

My mama came to the rescue with a custom that started with her daddy. She added a bit of coffee and a ton of sugar to warm milk to make it more appealing.

A woman ahead of her time, she beat Starbuck's to the punch by about 30 years, introducing the now-fashionable latte.

Modern-day parenting experts would cringe at such a practice, but I personally believe it gave us an academic edge over our peers. You wouldn't catch us dozing off in kindergarten.

Forget the milk and Oreos. For our after school snacks, we dined on lattes and scones (otherwise known as Mama's Tea Cakes). Yum!

* * * * * * * *

## Sweet Iced Tea

8 tea bags black tea
1-1/2 cups granulated sugar
4 cups water

Pour sugar into a 2-quart pitcher. Place water and tea bags in a large saucepan. Bring to a boil over medium-high heat. Remove from heat and let steep about 10 minutes. Discard tea bags and pour hot tea into pitcher containing sugar. Mix until all sugar is dissolved. Add tap water (or water and ice) to fill pitcher. Stir and refrigerate until ready to serve.

# Louisiana Lattes

2 cups milk
1 cup brewed coffee
1/4 cup granulated sugar (or to taste)
1 teaspoon vanilla extract

In a large saucepan, combine milk and coffee. Cook over medium heat until very hot. Stir in sugar and vanilla. Pour into cups. Makes 4 servings.


# Tea Cakes

2 cups self-rising flour
3/4 cup granulated sugar
3/4 cup shortening (or butter-flavored shortening)
2 large eggs
2 teaspoons vanilla extract

Preheat oven to 375°.

In a large bowl, blend flour and sugar.

Cut in shortening using a pastry blender or two knives.

Stir in eggs and vanilla and mix with hands until well blended.

Shape into 1-1/2-inch balls and press flat to about 1/4-inch thick on greased cookie sheet. Bake 10-12 minutes or until light brown. Do not over bake. Makes about ten 3-inch cakes. Serve warm with butter.

# Sweet Southern Lemonade

1 cup granulated sugar
1/2 cup hot water
1 cup freshly squeezed lemon juice
Cold water (about 6 cups)
1 lemon, sliced
Fresh mint leaves (optional)

Place sugar and hot water in a 2-quart pitcher and stir until sugar is dissolved.

Stir in lemon juice and enough cold water to fill container. Mix until well blended.

Pour into tall, ice-filled glasses. Add a slice of lemon. Garnish with mint, if desired.

# Mint Juleps

If you're lookin' for that Mint Julep Recipe—and I know you'd love to have one about now—you'll find it on page 44.

# Buttermilk Twist

Buttermilk plays a major role in Southern cooking for making biscuits, pancakes, cornbread, pies, cakes, salad dressings and even marinades.

I never could stand the taste of it for drinking, though. It makes my mouth pucker just thinking about it. But Mama liked to crumble warm cornbread into a tall glass of buttermilk and eat it for a snack.

We thought we'd seen it all when it came to cooking with buttermilk, until one hot summer evening when I was seven and our neighbor invited my family over for dessert.

"It's hotter than blue blazes," said Bonnie Lee. "Ya'll come on over after dinner. I'll drag out the ice cream freezer and make us a nice cold dessert."

No one owned electric ice cream makers back then. We packed ice and rock salt around the metal ice cream canister and used a hand crank to turn it.

The men took turns keeping the crank going while the ice cream froze. Since the handle jammed every now and then, we needed some weight on top to keep the bucket from jumping around all over the porch.

That's where the kids came in. We took turns sitting on a folded towel placed over the top of the bucket. It was the coolest seat on the porch. We knew our turn was up when our butts went numb and our teeth began to chatter.

But the hardest part about making ice cream was waiting for it to "ripen" after the cranking stopped.

The kids played hide-and-seek and chased lightning bugs, while the adults rocked and talked and fanned away the heat. It seemed like hours before that ice cream was hard enough for scooping, but Bonnie Lee finally pronounced it ready and passed out bowls of mouth-watering peach ice cream.

"This is wonderful," said Mama. "The peach flavor is luscious and the texture is so creamy. But it has a slight tang. Is it lemon juice?"

Bonnie Lee smiled. "It's buttermilk," she confessed.

"Buttermilk in ice cream?" Mama asked. "Land sakes, I never heard of such a thing."

I paused with a spoonful of ice cream in mid-air. My lips curled back at the thought of that sour tasting liquid.

Bonnie Lee's son hovered close to my elbow. "I'll be glad to eat yours if you don't want it."

My eyes narrowed. I clutched the bowl close to my chest. Not even buttermilk was going to come between me and that ice cream.

I shoveled in a mouthful and my taste buds began to tingle. "Yum," I said, scooping up some more. I couldn't eat that frosty confection fast enough.

"Slow down, Gloria Jean" said Mama. "You're gonna get brain freeze."

She was right, but it was worth every bite. "Ow!" I moaned. "Can I have some more, please? Ow!"

I was a buttermilk-eating fiend.

# Buttermilk Pie

3-1/2 cups granulated sugar
1/2 cup all-purpose flour
1 teaspoon salt
6 large eggs, beaten
1 teaspoon vanilla extract
3/4 cup butter or margarine, melted and cooled
    slightly
1 cup buttermilk
2 (9") pie shells

Preheat oven to 350°.

In a large bowl, mix together sugar, flour and salt.

In a separate bowl, blend melted butter, eggs and buttermilk. Stir egg mixture into dry ingredients until well blended.

Divide mixture evenly between two uncooked pie shells. Place pies on a cookie sheet and bake for one hour until the top is golden brown and filling is set.

Let cool completely before cutting.

## Looking For More Recipes Using Buttermilk?

Cherry Nut Loaf, page 32; Cornbread, page 100; Creamy Coleslaw, page 53, Fried Chicken, page 17; Homemade Biscuits, page 7; Hush Puppies, page 52; German Chocolate Cake, page 25; Peach Buttermilk Ice Cream, page 100; Texas Sheath Cake, page 82

# Peach Buttermilk Ice Cream

2 cups peeled and sliced ripe peaches (fresh, frozen &
    thawed, or canned & drained)
1 tablespoon lemon juice
1-1/4 cups granulated sugar, or to taste*
1/2 teaspoon ground cinnamon (optional)
2 cups heavy cream
1 cup buttermilk
1 teaspoon vanilla extract

Toss fresh peach slices with sugar, lemon juice and
cinnamon. Cover and refrigerate for at least 2 hours.
Mash or puree peaches in a blender. Mix puree with
cream, buttermilk and vanilla. Freeze according to ice
cream maker's instructions. Makes about 1 quart.

*If using canned peaches in heavy syrup, reduce sugar
to 1 cup or less, to taste.

# Buttermilk Cornbread

1-1/2 cups white cornmeal
3 tablespoons all-purpose flour
1 teaspoon salt
1 teaspoon baking soda
2 cups buttermilk
1 large egg, beaten
2 tablespoons bacon drippings or butter

Preheat oven to 450°. Sift dry ingredients into a large
bowl. Add buttermilk and egg, stirring until just
moistened. Melt drippings in an iron skillet or 9"
baking pan in the oven. Stir drippings into batter until
well blended. Pour batter into hot skillet. Bake 20 to
25 minutes or until done.

# Ya'll Come Back Now

Southerners are distinguished, not only by their distinctive accents, but their colorful sayings, as well.

Only someone born and raised in the South could tell you where "over yonder" is. If they say they'll be back "directly"—how long is that?

You'd best beware when asking for traveling directions. "Just down the road" might mean two blocks or 20 miles.

And Southerners are always "fixin' to" do something: make dinner, go to the store, or "box your ears!"

When my family returned to Louisiana for a visit one summer, Mama got a hankerin' to see a former, elderly neighbor. I tagged along, too. Lyda Mae was a hoot, and she always had a tasty treat baking in her oven.

We rang the doorbell and waited patiently for her to maneuver her walker to the door. Her weathered face lit up like Christmas when she saw us.

"Well butter my butt and call me a biscuit!" she yelled. "You two are a sight for sore eyes!"

She smothered us with bear hugs. "Glory Bee," she said to me, "you're growin' like a bad weed!" She ushered us into the house and, as is the custom with Southern hosts, her thoughts soon shifted to food.

"Come on back to the kitchen. I was just fixin' to heat up some lunch. Are you girls hungry?"

Do birds fly?

We settled around her tiny kitchen table with our plates loaded with spicy ham jambalaya and black eyed peas from Lyda Mae's garden. Just when we thought we couldn't eat any more, she set out a sweet potato pie and a plate of cookies. Life doesn't get any better.

"How's your mama?" asked Lyda Mae. "I haven't seen her in a coon's age."

"She's doin' fine," Mama said. "How're your boys?"

"Like two peas in a pod," Lyda Mae replied. "Both working at the refinery and fishin' on their days off. Rob finally married Linda Sue."

"The home coming queen?" asked Mama. "She was such a pretty little thing, riding on that float in the Home Coming Parade."

"Bless her heart," said Lyda Mae. "She blowed up like a blimp. She's big enough to BE the parade float now."

We shook our heads—poor Linda Sue.

Our afternoon visit covered all the usual neighborly topics: food, family, friends, food, weather and food.

As Mama and I prepared to leave, Lyda Mae bestowed more hugs and shed a few farewell tears.

"Ya'll come back now, ya' hear?"

# Ham Jambalaya

2 tablespoons vegetable oil
1/2 cup chopped onion
1/2 cup chopped green bell pepper
1/2 cup chopped red bell pepper
2 cloves garlic, minced (or 1/2 teaspoon garlic powder)
2 cups diced, fully-cooked ham
1 cup uncooked rice
1/2 teaspoon thyme
1/2 teaspoon salt
3-4 drops hot pepper sauce, or to taste
1 (14.5 oz.) can diced tomatoes
3/4 cup chicken broth (or 1 teaspoon chicken bouillon
   granules dissolved in 3/4 cup water)

Heat oil in a large saucepan. Add onion, bell pepper, and garlic. Cook, stirring occasionally, until vegetables are tender.

Add ham and rice. Stir until rice is well coated with oil. Add thyme, salt, hot sauce, tomatoes and chicken broth.

Cover and simmer until rice is tender and liquid has been absorbed, about 20 to 25 minutes.

# Fresh Black Eyed Peas

2-1/2 cups fresh or frozen black eyed peas
1/2 cup chopped onion
1 slice bacon
1/4 teaspoon garlic powder
Salt and ground black pepper to taste
Dash hot pepper sauce (optional)

Place all ingredients in a large saucepan.

Cover with about 2 inches of water on top and bring to a boil over medium-high heat.

Reduce heat and simmer 35-40 minutes or until peas are tender. Add additional water if needed to keep peas covered. Watch closely or they can burn.

Add a dash of hot sauce to the simmering peas if you like them spicy.

# Sweet Potato Pie

2 cups mashed, cooked sweet potatoes
1 cup granulated sugar
1/4 cup melted butter
2 large eggs
1 teaspoon vanilla extract
1/4 teaspoon salt
1 teaspoon ground cinnamon
1/4 teaspoon ground ginger
1/4 teaspoon ground nutmeg
1 cup evaporated milk
9-inch unbaked pie shell

Preheat oven to 350°.

In a large bowl, combine the potatoes, sugar, butter, eggs, vanilla, salt and spices. Mix thoroughly with an electric mixer. Add milk and beat until well blended.

Pour filling into pie shell and bake for 35 to 45 minutes, or until a knife inserted in the center comes out clean. Place pie on a rack and cool completely before serving.

# Peanut Butter Blossoms

1-3/4 cups all-purpose flour
1 teaspoon baking soda
1/2 teaspoon salt
1/2 cup granulated sugar
1/2 cup brown sugar, firmly packed
1/2 cup vegetable shortening
1/2 cup creamy peanut butter
1 large egg
2 tablespoons milk
1 teaspoon vanilla extract
48 Hershey's chocolate Kisses
Extra granulated sugar for rolling cookies

Preheat oven to 375°.

In a large bowl, combine flour, baking soda, salt, granulated sugar and brown sugar.

Add shortening, peanut butter, egg, milk and vanilla and beat on low speed until well blended.

Shape into 1" balls. Roll balls in granulated sugar. Place on a greased cookie sheet about 2" apart.

Bake for 10 minutes. Meanwhile, remove foil from chocolate kisses. Take cookies from the oven and press one kiss in the top of each cookie while cookies are still hot.

# Recipe Index

**Pies:**
Buttermilk Pie 99
Fried Fruit Pies 11
Kentucky Derby Pie 46
Pecan Pie 22
Sweet Potato Pie 105

**Side Dishes:**
Baked Beans 64
Black Eyed Peas 104
Coleslaw 53
Cornbread Dressing 69
Deviled Eggs 62
Green Beans 80
Green Tomatoes, Fried 91
Okra, Fried 58
Potato Pancakes 57
Potatoes, Scalloped 76
Potatoes, Skillet 57
Sweet Potato Casserole 71
Turnip Greens 65

**Salads:**
Chicken Salad 19
English Pea Salad 77
Fruit Salad 70
Potato Salad 65

**Sandwich Fillings:**
Egg Salad 41
Ham & Pineapple Spread 42
Pimiento Cheese Spread 42
Tuna & Apple Salad 41

# About the Author

Gloria Hander Lyons has channeled 30 years of training and hands-on experience in the areas of art, interior decorating, crafting and event planning into writing creative how-to books. Her books cover a wide range of topics including decorating your home, cooking, planning weddings and tea parties, crafting and self-publishing, plus humorous slice-of-life short stories.

Gloria has designed original craft projects featured in magazines, such as *Better Homes and Gardens, McCall's, Country Handcrafts* and *Crafts*. She teaches interior decorating and self-publishing classes at her local community college.

Visit her website for free craft ideas, decorating and party-planning tips and tasty recipes at: www.BlueSagePress.com.


# Ordering Information

To order additional copies of this book, make check or money order payable to Gloria Lyons and send to: Blue Sage Press, 48 Borondo Pines, La Marque, TX 77568.

Cost for this edition is $7.95 per book (U.S. currency only) plus $3.50 shipping and handling for the first book and $1.50 for each additional book shipped to the same U.S. address. Texas residents add 8.25% sales tax to total order amount.

To pay by credit card or get a complete list of books written by Gloria Hander Lyons, visit our website at:

www.BlueSagePress.com

# Other Books by Gloria Hander Lyons

- Easy Microwave Desserts in a Mug
- Easy Microwave Desserts in a Mug for Kids
- No Rules – Just Fun Decorating
- Just Fun Decorating for Tweens & Teens
- Decorating Basics: For Men Only
- Ten Common Home Decorating Mistakes & How to Avoid Them
- If Teapots Could Talk—Fun Ideas for Tea Parties
- The Super-Bride's Guide for Dodging Wedding Pitfalls
- Lavender Sensations: Fragrant Herbs for Home & Bath
- A Taste of Lavender: Delectable Treats with an Exotic Floral Flavor
- Designs That Sell: How to Make Your Home Show Better & Sell Faster
- Self-Publishing on a Budget: A Do-It-All-Yourself Guide
- The Secret Ingredient: Tasty Recipes with an Unusual Twist
- Hand Over the Chocolate & No One Gets Hurt: The Chocolate-Lover's Cookbook
- Flamingos, Poodle Skirts & Red Hots: Creative Theme Party Ideas
- Quick Gifts From the Kitchen: No Cooking Required
- 40 Favorite Impossible Pies: Main Dishes & Desserts
- Quick & Easy Sandwich Wraps
- A Taste of Memories: Comforting Foods From Our Past
- Pearls of Wisdom for Creating a Joyful Life
- What's Up With That? Humorous Short Stories About Life in Modern-Day America

For a complete list of books written by Gloria Hander Lyons, visit our website at:

www.BlueSagePress.com